ANOMALY

K.A. Emmons

www.kaemmons.com
ISBN: 978-1-7340146-0-0

ANOMALY

The Prequel to The Blood Race Trilogy

PROLOGUE

"DO YOU EVER HEAR strange, distant noises?"

"No."

"Do you ever experience strange feelings or crawling sensations just beneath your skin?"

"No. No, I don't think so…"

"Do you ever feel as though you are seeing things that other people can't see or don't seem to see?"

I looked down at my hands, curling my fingers into fists.

"No," I answered quietly. "No, I don't."

The woman sat in the chair across from me. I watched her jot things down on a clipboard. She had warm brown skin and wore her hair back in a tight bun. Her earrings jingled as her pen swept back and forth across the page.

"Do you ever feel confused as to whether something you're experiencing is real or imaginary?"

The wall clock ticked steadily for a moment as my eyes wandered back down to my hands. I didn't respond.

"Ion." She pulled in a steady breath. "I know it can be difficult, really, I do… but believe it or not, we are trying our best to help you."

Still I didn't look up. I didn't respond.

"But in order to help you, I need you to answer the question, Ion," she prodded gently. "Do you ever feel confused as to—"

"No." I severed her sentence, my voice like a cold, hard blade. "No, I don't."

I looked up to find her eyes locked on me. She studied my face for a moment before finally lowering her gaze back to her clipboard.

"Are your thoughts sometimes so strong that you can almost hear them?" she asked.

I felt hollow as I shook my head. As I said, "No," again.

"Do you ever feel as if there is some kind of force around you?"

"No."

"Do familiar surroundings sometimes seem strange, confusing, threatening or unreal to you?"

I shook my head. "No, never."

The small tidy office swelled with silence for a moment. I glanced past the social worker to the window at the other side of the room. Sunlight leaked in through the blinds to spill across the floorboards.

I closed my eyes, tipping my head back against the overstuffed couch. I could hear the pen scratching against the page. Finally, it stopped.

"Ion." Her voice was soft. "Ion, can you look at me, please?"

I was *so sick* of hearing that. My eyes were sore and heavy from lack of sleep, but finally I straightened up and looked at her.

"Do you ever feel that you are not in control of your own ideas or thoughts?" she asked gently.

The question echoed in my mind as the words sank in, leaving a cold, heavy feeling to settle in my stomach. I swallowed hard, my eyes shifting down to her hand resting against the clipboard, the pen hovering just above the page, waiting to ink whatever I was going to tell her in reply.

All the time, I thought.

"Never," I said.

I could tell by the look in her eyes that she didn't believe me. I could tell she knew I was bullshitting my way through this, but she scratched down what I had just said anyway.

"Ion, in your notebook—"

"I don't want to talk about what I wrote in there." My voice came out sharp, cutting her off. "It's nothing. It means nothing—"

"It's *important*." Her response was firm. "We *have* to talk about it."

I cursed under my breath, leaning forward to rest my elbows on my knees, pressing my fingertips to my forehead.

"You wrote that you were afraid of hurting the people you were living with," she said. "You felt responsible for the damage that had been done already—"

"Stop," I cut in again, the word coming out on the edge of a sharp breath. "Stop, please… Can we just talk about it later?"

There was a long silence again, filled up by the steady *tick, tick, tick* of the clock. I looked up just in time to see her pull out a black and white composition notebook. She split the covers between her hands and started leafing through the messy, inked pages.

"In your notes you mention meeting someone," she said finally, her voice quiet and steady. "And that he seemed to understand you when you spoke to him."

After a moment I blinked and cleared my throat. "Can you read what I wrote, please?"

She scanned the page again in silence before finally drawing a deeper breath.

"'I'm so scared… I'm scared of myself. I never thought I would say that, but I am,'" she read aloud. "'I wish I'd just told the old man everything—he's the only one who seems to get me, somehow. There's something about him… I feel like I can actually talk to him…'" She trailed off, her brown eyes flicking up to mine for a moment before she finished reading the rest.

"'But I'd just been so afraid that he would just push me away too if he knew the truth about me.'"

ONE

A FAMILIAR, PIERCING SCREAM cut through the quiet air like a knife. I froze, straightening, listening. Outside the window, tired trees swayed in the cool spring breeze, and for a moment the gentle whistling of the wind in those bare, scraggly arms was the only sound to penetrate the silence.

Then the scream came again. This time it was closer, forming a word: *Help*

I wrenched around to stare at the closed bedroom door, my fingers tightening around the pencil in my hand. Pushing back the chair, I crossed the room, pausing at the door to listen, pressing my ear to the chipped, painted wood. I held my breath.

The same word swung through the air, the same frantic voice. "Help! Help, he's bleeding!"

A door opened and slammed shut—the back door, I could tell by the creaking. *Boom, boom, boom*—footsteps across the floorboards followed.

"Momma, Momma, help—"

A quiet, strange yip interrupted.

Across the room, my eyes caught on my reflection in the mirror as I leaned against the door, listening. Wide blue eyes peeked out from under a chaos of messy dark brown hair to stare me down. The muscles in my jaw tightened as I swallowed.

I carefully slid my hand over the bedroom door and wrapped my fingers around the brass knob, twisting it. I opened the door just a crack—just enough to peek out into the hallway. It was dimly lit. I could see the staircase at the end of the hallway, and at the bottom of the stairs I could make out the coat rack.

More pounding footsteps. Another strained, animalistic yelp.

"He's bleeding!"

I opened the door a little wider and leaned cautiously out into the hallway.

I heard the sound of a chair pushing back across the floorboards, followed by curses blurted in the shape of Ava's voice. "Oh my God. How the—"

The squeak of hinges across the hall jerked my focus away from the conversation. The door across from mine swung open violently and hit the wall. Bleeping, static video game sounds and rusty light poured out into the hallway; Michael stood on the threshold, blotting out the mess in the room behind him. He clenched his hands around the door frame and narrowed his eyes as he studied me.

"What the hell's going on down there?" he demanded.

I looked back down the stairs, squinting at the front door, straining to decipher what was happening.

"Hey—hey, moron! I'm talking to you."

My gaze slid back to Michael. He was staring at me, still gripping the door frame. He was shirtless and wearing sweatpants. His short blond hair stuck up every which way.

"I'm not sure," I answered finally. "Why don't you go find out?"

Michael grunted. "I'll miss the bus."

"But what if something's wrong?"

He shrugged, his only response before recoiling into the muffled chaos of his room and slamming the door shut behind him. I stood there a moment longer, listening for sounds from downstairs. But this time there was only silence. Silence and, eventually, soft sobbing.

I stepped out into the hallway, leaving the bedroom door hanging open behind me. Unlike Michael's room, mine was empty with the exception of a desk scattered with half-finished homework. Holding my breath, I padded quietly down the stairs. I paused on the last step, listening.

The muffled sobs came and went, masking a watery voice.

"Can you help him? Momma—please—"

"Shhh, shh. Honey—just leave him here." Ava's voice. "You go on and get ready for school."

The small sobbing voice persisted, but the lumbering thud of footsteps behind me instantly snapped me out of my concentration. I flipped around to look behind me.

"Ion, what are you doing?" Ava's husband stood there in a white tank top and ripped pajama pants, a mug in one hand. He stank of black coffee and cigarettes. "Shouldn't you be getting ready for school?"

I opened my mouth to speak, shooting a quick glance down at myself. I was still just in boxers and a T-shirt.

"Uh, I was getting ready, sir. I just thought something might be..." I trailed off, shooting a glance in the direction of the living room, where I could still hear the muffled sobbing. "I thought something might be wrong."

Mr. Reeves took a sip of his coffee and frowned. "That's no concern of yours," he answered, rubbing his nose with the back of his hand. "Now you get upstairs and get your ass ready."

"But, sir, I heard Rachel crying—"

"I said *get* upstairs," he cut in firmly, stabbing a finger toward the second floor. "And tell Michael to—"

"No need," a new voice interrupted, the *thud, thud, thud* of footsteps coming down the stairs interrupting the conversation. "I don't need freakface to tell me to be on time for the bus."

He shoved me out of the way and jumped down the last couple of steps.

"Good." Mr. Reeves slapped his son on the backpack, then turned back to shoot me a look. "At least someone around here is."

I sighed. "Sir, just let me see if Rachel's alrigh—"

"Ion." He blurted my name like it was a curse, stepping closer now with his mug of coffee. From here I could smell that it wasn't just coffee. "You backtalk me one more time and I'm calling the goddamn agency."

I swallowed, then whirled around to pound back up the stairs, two at a time. Mr. Reeves muttered curses into his mug as he downed the rest of its contents.

I raced into my room and slammed the door shut behind me. I yanked open one of the dresser drawers and pulled out a pair of slightly too-big jeans, staggering into them as I clambered back over to the desk in front of the window. I froze when I glanced down to the place where the scattering of papers lay.

One out of the three assignments was missing: the one that had been on the top, the math assignment.

"Shit…" I quickly rifled through the papers, my eyes darting around frantically. "*Shit.*"

The rumble of an engine followed by the *pssstt* of air brakes wrenched me out of my thoughts. I leaned over the desk to look out the window. The long mustard-colored school bus idled at the sidewalk. The front door slammed downstairs, and a moment later I saw Michael dart across the front lawn. He paused when he reached the doors of the bus, squinting up at the window to flip me off before climbing aboard.

I stood there for a moment, listening to the grumbling of the bus's engine before it pulled away from the sidewalk and rolled down the street. I squeezed my eyes shut and kicked the leg of the desk.

Shit.

I collapsed into the desk chair, leaning forward to rest my head on my clenched fist. I sucked in a deep breath, only to blow it all back out again. This was the third time Michael had stolen my homework in the few months I'd been living with the Reeveses. The last time, Mr. Reeves had yelled at me so loudly the neighbors had called the police to complain about the noise.

I felt frozen, sitting there thinking about what would happen. I felt sick to my stomach considering it.

Why did I have to be here? Why did I have to be fourteen, four excruciatingly long years away from eighteen—and my long-awaited freedom?

My eyes stung as I squeezed them shut, listening to the quiet. The muffled garble of the television downstairs.

A warm, buzzing feeling tickled my fingertips. I sat up a little, opening my eyes. Spreading my palms in front of me, I looked down at my hands, swallowing back the tightness in my throat. My fingers trembled a little and my palms were sheathed in sweat.

What the hell…?

My heartbeat picking up, I grasped my left hand with my right, flexing my fingers, clenching them into a fist and spreading them out again. I took a deep breath and slowly picked up the pencil I'd been using, pinching it securely between my forefinger and thumb, trying to force my hand to steady.

Instead, the pencil only trembled in my grip, first just a little, then more and more violently until it wriggled out of my grip and dropped to the floor.

Sucking in a frustrated breath, I hunched forward on the desk again, clenching my head in my hands. I breathed for a moment in silence before leaning down to pick up the pencil. It slipped out of my fingers again. Frustrated now, I tried once again to clasp it, but it only flicked away from my grasp.

I pushed back the chair to get up. I bent down to grab the stupid pencil, but my trembling fingers froze, hovering just above it. Slowly, trembling about as much as my hands were, one end of the pencil peeled up off the floor and hovered in midair.

My eyes widened as I lurched backward, tripping and falling over my own two feet; the pencil dropped to the floor again with a clatter.

I scrambled backward on my ass, blinking and gulping air.

Holy shit. Am I hallucinating, or did it actually just…?

I could hear muffled voices downstairs: Rachel's sobbing tangled with the arguing voices of Mr. and Mrs. Reeves. A moment later those voices faded out to one.

"Ion, you missed the bus," Ava yelled up the stairs. "Come on… I'll give you a ride. Hurry up."

My voice was too thick in my throat to reply. My back hit the wall as I reached the other side of the room. The jolt was enough to knock the wind out of me and yank me back down to earth.

"Ion?" she yelled again after a moment. "Ion, are you alright up there?"

I opened my mouth and closed it again. The pencil rolled to a stop on the floor. I stared at it for a moment before looking back down at my hands. They were still shaking.

"Y-y-yeah," I called back, my voice cracking a little. "I-I'm fine. I'll be right down."

TWO

AVA REEVES WAS ALRIGHT. She was a short lady with dyed red hair and premature wrinkles from smoking. She drove a pickup truck and only played the eighties hits station on the radio. She wore a fleece sweater with horses on it almost every time she left the house. This time she was wearing it zipped up all the way as she climbed into the driver's seat and rubbed her hands together.

"Frickin' cold for spring," she muttered, slamming the door shut.

I glanced over at her. "Rachel not going to school today?"

Mrs. Reeves shook her head. "No."

She twisted around to look over her shoulder as she backed out of the dirty, snowy driveway and onto the main road lined with houses that all looked the same. I stared out the grimy windshield for a few moments.

"What happened?" I asked finally.

Ava took a deep breath, but then just bit her lip. "People are careless assholes, Ion, that's what happened," she said finally. She sighed, flexing her fingers on the worn steering wheel as we came to a stop at a traffic light. "I told Rachel not to let Gabe wander, but–"

"That dog down the street?" I asked, a sinking feeling already settling in my gut.

Ava nodded. "He attacked Gabe."

"Shit…"

"They never keep that damn animal on a leash," she continued.

"What about Gabe?" I asked. "Is he gonna be alright?"

The light turned green again, and Ava leaned into the gas pedal, keeping her gaze fixed on the road beyond the grimy windshield. "I bandaged him as best I could, but I'm sure his leg is broken."

The tone of her response commanded that no further questions be asked, so I kept my mouth shut. We drove in silence. I leaned my head against the window and watched the dirty snow blur past until we turned into the high school parking lot. The building was an ugly brick one with premature cling-on Easter decorations stuck to the windows.

Ava pulled the truck up along the sidewalk and shifted into park. She blew out a tired sigh and turned to look at me. "This is your stop."

My stomach sank as I jerked the passenger door open. "Thanks for the ride. I'm sorry I missed the bus."

Ava nodded absentmindedly. "Just don't let it happen again."

I gave her a weak thumbs-up as I climbed out of the truck, shouldering my backpack. I slammed the rusted door shut and stood there, watching as she pulled away from the curb and rolled off. I took a long shaky breath before turning to walk to the door, cursing each of my reluctant steps.

Everything was the same here, the same as it had been in all the other towns. My backpack was loaded down with the weight of every punch and every shove—a collection I added to with every place I stayed. Every time I walked through those doors and breathed in that school smell, déja vu spilled down on me like a tidal wave. It was always the same no matter where I went.

By the time I got to my first class, I was late. The teacher, a pretty Asian lady named Ms. Wu, looked up from her desk when I stepped in.

"Ion, you're late," she said, pointing out what was painfully obvious. Chairs creaked as students turned to face the back of the classroom.

I swallowed, my face going red, my voice bracing in my throat, refusing to make its entrance.

"Take a seat, please."

I shuffled to my desk and sat down. I barely heard anything that was being said, but when I looked up, I caught Michael shooting me a hard stare from the other side of the room. I tried to listen to what Ms. Wu was saying, but it was as if her voice grew more and more distant.

No matter how hard I tried, I couldn't focus: every time I closed my eyes, all I could see was that pencil hovering inches above the floor. I took a deep breath and pinched my eyes shut. I flexed my fingers into a fist, then spread them out again. My palms were starting to sweat.

Was I seeing things? Was I imagining it all?

What the hell is wrong with me?

"Ion, maybe you can answer this one." The muffled voice funneled into earshot once again.

I squeezed my hands back into fists; I could feel my face glowing red again. Ms. Wu was gazing across the classroom at me, one dark eyebrow arched.

I cleared my throat. "I'm sorry. I, uh—I didn't hear the question."

Her facial expression remained the same for a moment before finally she gave a single nod. "Ion, I'd like to see you after class, please."

I heard a couple of students laugh quietly. After that, everything faded once again to silence, to the persistent ringing in my ears as my brain rehashed the eerie events of that morning.

I tried to stay focused while class dragged on for what seemed like hours. My stomach dropped when class finally ended and everyone filed out of the room, leaving me to reluctantly approach Ms. Wu's desk alone. Her eyes were soft and concerned.

"Everything alright, Ion?" she asked. "Is there anything you want to talk about?"

I shook my head. "Everything's fine."

Her eyebrows lifted slightly as she leaned forward to rest her elbows on her desk. "Do you want to explain why you didn't turn in your homework assignment, then?"

I thought about it for a moment, glancing down at the floor. "I lost it," I admitted finally. "Sorry."

There was a long pause before Ms. Wu finally sighed. "Ion, you've been attending school here for a few months now," she said. "Haven't you found anything that you like yet?"

I shrugged. "I like track a little. Running."

"What is it you like about running?"

"I like being outside," I answered quietly. "Climbing things, jumping over obstacles—you know, like parkour."

Ms. Wu pressed her lips into a little smile. "And what is it you like about parkour?"

I looked at her questioningly, trying to figure out what she was probing for. Finally, I just shrugged again and reached up to rub the back of my neck. "I guess I like the way it makes me feel."

"How's that?"

"Fast," I answered after a moment of consideration. "Free."

Ms. Wu seemed to psychoanalyze my answer for a moment before straightening up. "Ion, maybe you should try going for a run before you sit down to do homework. Especially math."

"Because I'm flunking?"

"Because you could be doing better," she corrected me. "I know you could; you have the potential. You just need to get into the right frame of mind."

She shuffled some papers around, then tapped a few into a stack before stapling them and handing them to me. "Give it another shot, alright?"

I looked at her for a moment before cautiously taking the papers. "Alright. Alright, thanks."

She stretched her lips into an encouraging smile, and I turned and walked out of the classroom. The hallways were alive and chaotic with noise. I wove my way through the throng until I reached my locker. I'd just begun to open it when a hand slammed the door shut.

Startled, I shifted my eyes up to meet Michael's. He stood in front of me with his arm braced over the door to my locker. His slate-gray eyes were narrowed.

"What did you tell her?" he asked, tipping his head back to look down his nose at me. He was barely taller than I was.

"That would be none of your business," I replied flatly, reaching for the door to my locker once again. "Now get the hell out of my way."

A bone-on-bone thud sizzled through my arm as Michael blocked my hand with his fist, stepping up to my face this time, leaning close enough that I caught the scent of his stale breath.

"If you say one goddamn word to my dad about what really happened to that assignment, I'll smash your teeth through the back of your skull, weirdo," he muttered, still scrutinizing me through narrowed eyes. "My dad would never believe a word you say anyway."

I stared at him blankly for a moment, then gave a brisk nod. "I've noticed."

Michael's expression steeled. "Ever think about why that is?"

"No, not really," I replied flatly. "Now *get out* of my way."

He shoved me backward.

"No one listens to you because no one wants you here, Ion," he went on, as if I hadn't even spoken. "You're just a piece of garbage no one wants—a stray that gets tossed from one place to the next because no one gives a shit about you." He gave me another firm shove backward, and this time the papers in my hand spilled to the floor.

Michael drove me back against the wall and held me there, looking square into my eyes.

"No one wants a freak like you, Ion," he hissed, spit flying out of his mouth with the venomous words. "*No one.*"

For a moment, everyone and everything else seemed to fade, the world around me crashing to a halt, mute, just as it had in class. There was no sound, just the *thud, thud, thud* of my own racing heart as that same strange, vibrating feeling filled the palms of my hands and trickled into my fingertips.

Everything slowed down, almost freezing completely as my fingers clenched into fists. I stared back into Michael's eyes for a moment.

Then everything snapped back to normal speed as my arm slung back and my fist landed on his jaw. The force threw him backward, across the hall and into the row of lockers with a bang.

THREE

MICHAEL HUNCHED ON THE FLOOR, leaning up against the lockers for a moment, stunned and gasping for air. The hall had quieted; everyone had stopped what they were doing to stare. I wasn't about to stick around for Michael's reaction—I was already turning to leave, but even that second of hesitation had been one second too long.

Michael lunged belligerently for my legs, snatching me by the ankles. I went down fast, and my face bashed into the hard linoleum. Pain sizzled through my head, and noise erupted around me. I attempted to claw my way up to my knees, but I felt the full weight of a body drop on top of mine, knocking the air out of me.

As he wrenched me around onto my back, I saw only a burning blur from the fluorescent lights above before Michael's fist slammed into my face. Pain shot through my right eye socket and up into my aching skull. My eyes welled and my vision blurred.

Michael punched me again and again. I swung for his face, but I could barely see. My hands were still shaking uncontrollably, and I could hear kids shouting through my muffled sense of hearing.

Finally, with every ounce of strength I had, I levered myself up with my elbows, jolting my torso enough to send Michael sprawling to the floor. I jumped to my feet and bolted, swimming through the crowd as Michael roared after me. I heard one of the classroom doors fly open and a voice demanding to know what was going on.

I didn't stop or even look back. I just kept running.

Dodging kids, I stumbled down the stairwell and through the doors. When I was outside again, a stiff blast of cold air slapped me in the face. Everything was blurry and wavering around me as I wiped the tears from my eyes with my forearm and picked up my pace, darting out of the parking lot and taking off down the sidewalk.

My lungs burned with every breath I took as my sneakers pounded against the cement.

What the hell just happened? How the hell was I able to punch him that hard? Did I really hit him hard enough to throw him across the hall like that?

My hands trembled even as these questions churned in my mind.

I ran harder, taking a sharp turn onto the side road that led to the state park—down to the lake. I slowed up only when pines and birches had risen up along either side of the road. For what felt like the first time, I drew a breath.

The echoes of the shouting voices ringing in my ears slowly faded away to the still, soft stirring of the wind in the trees. The cool atmosphere was fragrant with melting snow and thawing earth. I turned off the road after a while and cut through the patch of woods that skirted the lake, trying to ignore the pain still throbbing in my face as my fingertips brushed the rough bark of pines and the smooth, peeling skin of birches. Overhead, the leaves swirled, danced and stilled again. A robin sang somewhere close by.

I closed my eyes and listened, placing one hand over my eye. It was already pretty swollen.

I scooped up a handful of snow and held it to my face as I kept walking, putting one foot in front of the other until I reached the beach, where the waves were gently lapping, filling the quiet with the soft *swish, swish, swish* of icy water.

I stopped at the tree line for a moment, leaning against a slouching pine. The snow melted and dribbled down my face and under the collar of my shirt, raising chill bumps as I stared out at the shimmering water. The overcast sky had shed its skin to a shade of robin's-egg blue, and it reflected across the surface of the lake like scattered shards of broken glass.

There was no one on the beach; I was alone with the lapping water and the howling of my thoughts, which seemed to chant Michael's words:

You're just a piece of garbage no one wants... no one wants... no one wants...

I stepped away from the trees and walked across the beach a little ways, stopping to sit down on an old log the lake had coughed up.

What Michael had said was nothing new. The words were old and tired—in fact, I was so used to them I was surprised they still hurt.

Maybe they just cut because I sometimes caught myself wondering whether or not they were true. Maybe no one did want me—not even my parents. Maybe that was why things had always been this way—getting tossed from one foster family to the next. At least that was what they called it—"family" it wasn't. I met new people all the time and then left them to move on to the next. I didn't get to know anyone and no one knew me. Sometimes I felt like I didn't even know myself.

Ion Jacobs. That was what I was called, but it wasn't the name my parents had given me; it was just a name the orphanage had slapped on when they found me. It wasn't a real name. Sometimes I felt like it matched the unreality of the rest of me, confirming my status as a nobody.

I closed my eyes, gritting my teeth as I swallowed back the fresh waves of pain ebbing through my face.

I felt sick to my stomach when I started considering how Mr. Reeves would react when Michael told him about what I had done. He would call the agency for sure, there was no doubt in my mind about that, but I was worried about more than just that. He'd already been drinking when we left for school, and being jobless left him home with his booze all day while Ava worked. He was like a dark sky as it was when he was sober, but when he was drunk, he was a hurricane.

I didn't want to go back to the house. Not until I knew Ava was home. Mike Reeves would notice my shiner right away and ask me about it. The school had probably already been in contact with him about the fight.

Taking a deep breath of cool air, I tried to push these thoughts to the back of my mind. Despite the cold, I slid out of my sneakers and peeled off my socks. The frozen ground stung my feet as soon as my skin made contact with it. Still holding my aching face in my hand, I stood to walk to the water's edge.

Shivers rushed down my spine with every step I took until the quiet water lapped against my toes, raising the hairs on the back of my neck and arms. The freezing water made me forget about the throbbing pain in my face for a moment as it curled around my ankles, seeming to coax me out into the depths.

What would happen if I just kept walking until the water was over my head? Would anyone even notice or care if I vanished?

"Little cold for a swim, isn't it?"

The robust voice was so sudden I nearly jumped out of my skin as I whipped around in the direction it had come from. A tall, scraggly old man stood about ten yards off, wearing a hoodie, torn jeans and a baseball cap. He shielded his eyes with one hand, and his other arm was loaded with driftwood. He squinted at me curiously.

"I'm not," I yelled back. "I'm not going for a swim. I just wanted to feel… the water."

I just wanted to feel. That was what I'd really wanted to say. But that never sounded normal.

The old man stood there, squinting at me a moment longer before stooping to pick up another piece of driftwood. "Cold, isn't it?"

I bobbed my head in a quick nod as he made his way over, his eyes scanning the sand for scattered driftwood. He stopped when he got closer and peered at me curiously. I could see his eyes now; they were bright blue and crested with wrinkles.

"You hurt?"

I became aware of my swelling eye once again. I shook my head, stepping back out of the water. "It's nothing."

"Don't look like nothing."

"It's *nothing*," I insisted. "Just a fight."

I turned and walked back to my shoes, collapsing back down onto the log. The old man continued picking up wood, and for a moment the silence swelled with the shushing of the waves.

"Did you give back as good as you got?" he asked.

I glanced up from brushing the sand off my feet. "I'd say so, yeah."

"You start it?"

I shook my head, then hesitated. "Looking back, maybe I did… I don't know anymore."

I started tugging on my socks.

"Someone at school?"

"Not just school." I winced as another stab of pain shot through my head. "He's the son of the people I live with. Foster home."

The old man said nothing, but after a moment he bowed his head in a single nod. "I see."

"I came here because I didn't want to go back, not yet." I shoved my feet back into my shoes. "I just… I dunno."

"Gotta be rough to go home to the parents of the kid you just decked."

I grunted. "I'll be the one to get decked this time, when he sees my shiner—he'll know I was the one who punched Michael."

The old man frowned. "You'd better take care of that eye, then."

I grunted. "Swelling doesn't go down that fast."

The old man straightened up, adding a few more weathered sticks to the pile in his arm. "I made camp just a little ways down the beach. I have a first aid kit there."

"Are you homeless?"

He shook his head, smiling a little. "Earth is my home."

"So you're a hippie, then," I concluded.

He laughed a little. "Call me what you wish." He jerked his head for me to follow, and I trailed him down the beach, holding my head in my hand.

Eventually we came to a driftwood hut with the ashy remains of a fire just outside. I shot the old man a glance as he dropped the wood into a clattering heap.

He gestured to one of the large logs arranged around the ash pile. "Have a seat."

I sat down on the edge of the log and watched curiously as he pushed aside the canvas flap that covered the hut's entrance and ducked inside. I glanced out over the lake, squinting to see in the bright sunlight. A hawk swooped through the air and plunged into the cold water, emerging with a shimmering fish in its beak.

The canvas swished again, snapping my attention back to my surroundings.

"Here." The old man tossed me an ice pack. "That'll help."

I snatched it in midair and pressed it to my face. "Thanks."

Shit, that hurts.

The old man didn't sit down. He went over to the pile of driftwood and picked up a few sticks, then carried them over to the side of the hut to start laying them up on the roof.

"So you live out here?" I asked finally.

"Yep."

"I didn't think they allowed people to live on the beach like this," I said. "No one's ever given you a hard time about it?"

The old man shook his head. "Not yet."

I watched him arrange the driftwood for a while.

"How the hell do you survive out here? It's freezing at night," I pointed out, shifting the ice pack.

"The fire's warm." He grabbed a few more sticks. "Ice feel good?"

"Feels like shit," I told him.

He smiled a little, walking over to the side of the hut again. I turned to look back out at the hawk swooping and diving through the air.

"Wish I could do something like this," I muttered after a moment, more to myself than to the old man. "Live out here on my own. No one to push me around and make me go places I don't want to..."

I sighed and looked down at the ground for a moment. The old man didn't respond right away. After a moment he circled back around to the pile, but this time he didn't pick up more sticks. He sat down on the log across from me.

"Take the ice pack away for a second," he said.

My brow furrowed, but after a moment's hesitation I did what he'd asked. I could barely open my eye at this point. The old man squinted, studying my face intently for a moment, saying nothing. I could practically feel my skin burning from the intensity of his gaze.

Then, abruptly, he stood. I squinted up at him, watching as he once again picked up a few sticks and circled around to the side of the hut to strategically add them to the shack's construction.

I placed the ice pack back on my face and shifted it a little; the ice must have been working its magic, because already my eye socket throbbed a little less.

"You mind if I just hang around for a little while?" I asked finally.

The old guy didn't stop working. He shrugged a shoulder as he tossed another piece of driftwood up onto the roof. "You know how to build a fire?"

I hesitated, then shook my head.

The old guy tipped his head toward the ashy smudge. "Then you'll have to learn."

FOUR

I LEARNED HOW TO light a fire by rubbing two sticks together, just like in those survivor shows.

I stayed with the old guy on the beach for a few hours. I warmed my hands by the fire, and eventually, when my face felt normal again, I helped him reinforce the walls of the driftwood hut with the pieces he'd gathered. My brain still sloshing from the fight, I never thought to ask his name.

When the sun had lowered in the sky, I knew it was time to head back to the Reeveses'.

"You always around here?" I asked, setting the ice pack down on the log and getting to my feet to stretch.

The old guy prodded the burning logs with a stick. "Not always, no."

"Thought you said you lived here?"

"I do for now," he replied.

"So you've lived other places?"

He seemed to consider my question for a moment before switching his gaze up to mine. "Haven't you?"

I shrugged. "Been a few places, I guess."

He continued to stoke the flames. "So Earth is your home too, then?"

I shook my head. "Nah, I just don't have a home."

"Everyone has a home," he corrected me, setting the stick down. "If they know where they come from."

The corners of my lips twitched into a mirthless grin. "Guess that's my problem, then."

The old guy asked nothing else, and after a moment I turned to squint out over the lake. "Guess I'd better get going," I said at last, taking a few steps away from the flicker of the fire. "It's gonna be dark soon. Thanks again for the ice."

The old guy didn't say anything. He adjusted his ball cap and bobbed his head in a nod.

I walked away from that fire with a strange feeling in my gut. Not until I reached the dirt road that wound through the woods did it cross my mind that I should have asked the homeless guy what his name was.

Oh well. The chances were pretty slim that I'd ever see him again.

I cut through the woods out to the main road, leaving the lake and the clusters of quiet pines and birches behind. I picked up my pace to a run and sprinted down the streets, dodging the traffic until I reached the sleepy street where the Reeveses lived. I slowed up when their house came into view. The windows were ripe with warm tungsten light, but the rusty pickup was still absent from the driveway. Ava wasn't home yet.

Shit.

Inching my way to the house, I snuck around the back, ducking beneath the windows. I was about to break out from the cover of the house to make a mad dash for the back door when I heard drifting voices in the backyard. I halted, flattening myself against the side of the house, and shuffled closer to peer around the corner.

In the wash from the porch light, I could just make out the shape of Mr. Reeves as he lifted a cigarette to his mouth, igniting a glimmer of tired amber. His son stood beside him, his face half tucked away in shadow, half doused in the low light.

"He could have killed me, Dad." Michael's voice was laced with rage. "Don't you get that? I thought he broke my jaw!"

Mike Reeves grunted, and a moment later thin wisps of smoke feathered up into the air. "You mean to tell me that you couldn't give that scrawny little bastard back as good as he gave?"

"Oh, I punched him, Dad—a few times. I tackled him to the floor," he explained. "You'll see; you'll see when he comes crawling home with a black eye."

Mr. Reeves took another long drag, then slowly shook his head. "He'd better. Because no son of mine is going to be incapable of knocking down some scrawny little no-name asshole."

"Dad, I beat him good, I'm telling you!"

I folded back behind the house, panting for breath, my heart thundering in my chest.

Why the hell was I here? Why was I here when fifty percent of the Reeves family hated my guts—couldn't wait to see me come walking in with a busted face to affirm that Michael had been successful in gaining the upper hand?

I tipped my head back and let out a long sigh, watching my breath roll away from me in a small disintegrating puff. It came apart in the air and vanished to nothing. I'd thought about doing the exact same thing only hours earlier. What had stopped me?

It didn't matter anymore. I'd have to face the humiliation. I had no other choice.

It was my fault, really. I'd thrown the first punch.

Such a bad move. Why had I done it? It hadn't even felt like a conscious decision… More like something that had welled up inside me and overtaken me without my permission; it was like there'd been nothing I could do to stop it.

Shivering in the cold night air, I lowered my gaze down to my hands, studying the vague shapes of my fingers in the dark.

I thought of the pencil.

I thought of the way my hands had shaken in class.

I thought of how I'd punched Michael—sent him flying backward into the row of lockers.

Standing there in the raw, cold darkness, I couldn't shake the strange feeling that was welling up inside me, that same warm, trembling sensation.

What the hell is happening to me?

The sudden grumbling of a truck's engine tugged me out of my thoughts. Bright headlight beams swept across the house and came to a stop. I could hear the bassy undertones of music drifting from the vehicle's interior for a moment before Ava cut the engine and swung the door open.

I shuffled out from the shadows and stepped into the driveway. She noticed me right away, sucking in a sharp breath as I emerged from the shadows.

"God, Ion, you startled me." Her words rushed out. "What are you doing out here this late?"

I opened my mouth, then stopped. She didn't wait for a response; she was already shivering and gesturing for me to follow her to the front door.

"Come on. You can explain inside." She held the door for me. Reluctantly, I caught it and stepped in after her.

The door slamming shut was Mike Reeves's trigger.

"Ava," his voice boomed from the kitchen, "get in here."

I kicked myself. We were both about to get put through the wringer, and it was all my fault; all because I'd chosen to pick a fight with Michael. Mrs. Reeves had yet to turn and look me in the face.

Damn it.

Ava set down her keys. "What's going on?"

Michael was leaning against the counter with his arms folded over his chest as I trailed Ava into the kitchen, standing behind her like she was a shield.

"That boy of yours attacked my son," Mr. Reeves stated, like it was gospel, jabbing his finger at his wife. "This is the final straw, Ava."

"What the hell are you talking about?" Ava shot back. "What's Ion done?"

Mr. Reeves made a sweeping gesture with his hand, almost spilling his glass of whiskey. "Turn around and look at the boy, for Christ's sake."

He hadn't even looked at me himself yet; no one had. I was still standing on the threshold behind Ava, tucked back in the low light. Everything seemed to slow as she turned to look at me. My throat tightened and I swallowed hard.

Ava's blue eyes narrowed as they flickered over my face; then she looped an arm around my shoulders and tugged me into the kitchen.

"What exactly are you talking about?" Her tone grew demanding. "I see nothing wrong with him."

My heart began to pound again as Mr. Reeves's bloodshot eyes finally focused on mine over the rim of his glass. They widened a little and he swallowed hard.

Michael cursed, slamming his heel back into the cabinet. "There's no way! I beat his goddamn face in—"

"You *what*?" Mrs. Reeves cut in before her stepson could finish, throwing a swift glance between the two of us.

Michael's face froze, both his parents silently waiting for different kinds of explanations. Finally, his father answered for him.

"Go up to your room," he growled. "And stay there until you feel like telling the truth about who you really fought with!"

"But, Dad, it was Ion!" Michael's voice was frantic, his eyes wild now. "I swear, I'm not lying!"

"I said go to your room, now!" Mr. Reeves roared, his drink sloshing in his glass as he jabbed his finger violently in the direction of the stairs.

Michael's bruised face twisted and steeled as his eyes fixed on mine, narrowing with hatred. Storming the length of the room, he shoved me out of the way and pounded up the stairs. Mrs. Reeves shouted reprimands after him, but I barely heard.

Mr. Reeves started yelling at me, but then his attention shifted to his wife as she stepped in front of me to shout back into her husband's face. I slipped back into the shadows of the dimly lit living room, crossing it and vanishing down the hallway. When I reached the bathroom, I slammed the door shut behind me and locked it.

For a moment I just stood there in the dark, listening to the muffled argument. Then I flipped on the light and stepped up to the mirror. My heart lifted to my throat as I studied the reflection of my own face.

My own completely normal-looking face.

"What the…" My voice faded in my throat as I reached up to trace my forefinger along the skin that only an hour ago had been puffy, swollen, and most likely black and blue. Unblemished flesh had replaced my battle scars.

I leaned closer, pressing my fingers to my face. My dark brown hair was a messy thatch straying down over my blue eyes.

How is this possible? Had my bruising really been so minor?

There was no way. I'd felt like total shit only hours ago—there was no way I'd walk away from something like that unscathed. Yet my face looked fine now.

I turned on the cold tap and filled my cupped hands with icy water to splash over my face.

The cool liquid was like a slap as it rushed over my skin, then dripped down my neck and back. It reminded me of the cold, swirling water around my feet that morning.

Strength ebbing away from me, I leaned forward, resting my forehead against the mirror. I watched as drops of water rolled off my face and fell into the basin, tracing down the drain. The shouting began to escalate downstairs in the kitchen. I squeezed my eyes shut.

You're just a piece of garbage no one wants…

When the fighting in the kitchen faded to outside, I crept back downstairs. Snagging a glass from the kitchen cabinet, I went to the sink and filled it with water. As a stood there listening to the shouting outside, I started noticing something else—something softer in the background, a muffled sound I couldn't quite make out at first, but the longer I listened, the more I heard. Finally I identified it.

Sobbing.

Draining the glass and setting it in the sink, I crossed the room quietly to slip into the adjacent hallway. I followed the sound of the quiet crying until I reached the closed door with chipped paint and horse stickers plastered all over it. Light drizzled out from the crack under the door.

I stood there for a moment, leaning against the door, listening. Then I knocked softly.

The sobbing stopped. I heard a few sniffles.

"Go away!" a watery voice yelled from inside.

I leaned a little closer to speak softly into the crack between the door and the frame. "Rachel, it's me."

There was a long silence.

Finally, I pushed the door open just enough to slip inside. The room was lit in shades of multicolored tungsten light; Rachel had one of those floor lamps with multiple bulbs and different colored shades. The carpet was thick and cluttered with toys. Like a crescendo to the chaos, she was seated on the floor in the middle of it all, hunkered down in front of a lump wrapped in a fleece blanket.

Rachel was one of the tiniest seven-year-old girls I'd ever seen.

Her back was to me, but I could tell she was crying; her small body trembled as she drew shaky breaths. Her long blond hair trailed down her back.

"Hey." My voice came out soft as I shut the door behind me. "What's wrong?"

Rachel didn't answer. Her tiny body only trembled more fiercely as she shook her head.

I picked my way through the toys, clearing a spot on the floor with my foot to sit down beside her.

"Hey." I hushed her. "Come on... It's okay..."

"No," she sniffed, still shaking her head. "No–it's–it's not..."

Finally, my attention turned to the mound of blankets. I already knew what I'd find there before I even peeled back the fleece blanket to reveal the small fluffy head. The small, shivering terrier mutt lay still, moving only its eyes to look at me. Its front leg was wrapped in makeshift bandages.

I sucked in a shallow breath and let it out again. I gently placed a hand on Rachel's shoulder. She brushed it away, fiercely wiping her tears away. She turned to look up at me with large watery blue eyes. When she finally spoke, her voice was so quiet I almost couldn't make out the words.

"Do you think he's gonna be okay, Ion?"

I pulled in a narrow breath, my mind racing for a reply that wouldn't come fast enough. Finally I just sighed and shook my head.

"I don't know, Rachel," I answered her quietly, looking back down at the tiny trembling dog wrapped in blankets. "He looks like he's… in a lot of pain."

Rachel sucked back tears and rubbed her eyes, her lips twisting into a grieved, trembling frown. "Can you make him better, Ion?"

I bit my lip, looking from Gabe to Rachel. "I wish I could," I told her softly.

She sniffed hard, tears welling in her eyes again; this time she just covered them with her hands, like she was ashamed to cry in front of me.

"The dog down the street grabbed his leg," she explained, her voice cracking. "I asked Momma if it was broken, but she wouldn't tell me."

I said nothing. I pulled back the blanket a little farther, examining the rest of Gabe's tiny shaking body. His wiry coat was splotched with blood and dirt. When I gently grazed his bandaged leg with my fingertips, his jaws snapped at my hand and he let out a high-pitched yelp.

I didn't know a lot about animals, but it was more than probable that his leg was broken. I could tell by the way Ava had talked about it that morning that they didn't have the money to take him to the vet. This was the beginning of the end for Rachel's dog. It was just a matter of time.

I wasn't about to be the one to tell her that, but I couldn't bring myself to lie to her, either.

"Look." I heaved a sigh, turning to look at her. "Maybe… maybe he just needs to rest."

Rachel steadied her breath, sniffing back tears as she met my gaze. "You think so?"

I hesitated, then nodded a little. "And I think you need some rest too. So why don't you let me sit up with Gabe, and you take a little break and lie down for a while?"

Rachel tilted her head to the side, seeming unsure about the idea. But then, finally, she surrendered a nod.

"Just for ten minutes," she answered quietly.

I nodded and forced a reassuring smile for her sake.

I watched as she crossed the room to climb wearily into her unmade mess of pink sheets and blankets, her tearstained face matching them in color. Tears rolled down her cheeks as she squeezed her eyes shut.

FIVE

I COULD STILL REMEMBER the first time I'd finally broken down and asked someone where I'd come from—how they'd found me. It had been a nice social worker from the agency, and the troubled look in her eyes had contrasted her fake smile.

"You were left in our care, Ion." That was how she'd put it.

I'd been too young to understand what that implied—that I'd been abandoned. It wasn't until much, much later that I'd finally gotten a real answer out of someone.

Somewhere along a winding, back-country dirt road, someone had spotted a car crash in the woods. The tire marks had left messy streaks from the road down into the brush, like arrows pointing to the wreckage: an older car with a smashed-out windshield. There was no one in the driver's seat, no passengers—just a sleeping infant in the backseat, naked and wrapped in a thin blanket. Even after extensive investigation, they never figured out who the driver was. It remained a complete and bewildering mystery.

It was eerie, haunting, and it made me different from the other kids somehow, even though they didn't know about it—no one except the workers at the agency did. Once known, it couldn't be unknown; I could feel its stranglehold around my throat when I was around other people, reminding me that I was different from them, strange. Tainted.

My ambiguous past haunted me, stroking its long cold fingers over my brain as I sat there in the stillness enshrouding Rachel's bedroom, interrupted only by the muffled arguments of her parents until at last it climaxed in smashing glass and a slamming door. A moment later, the truck rumbled to life and rolled out of the driveway, followed by Ava's angry sobs from the kitchen.

I closed my heavy eyelids for a moment, just sitting there. Just listening. Beneath it all I could hear Rachel softly breathing where she had fallen asleep in an exhausted pile.

I felt bad for her. She lived in such chaos. She had Michael Reeves for a half-brother, and if that wasn't already bad enough, she was about to lose the one friend she had: her slobbering mutt Gabe. He seemed to be the only thing to bring a smile to her face when she came home from school.

The soft sounds of footsteps in the hallway caught my attention. A moment later the door softly creaked open. I turned to look over my shoulder just as Ava peeked her head in. Her eyes were red from crying, but she managed a weak smile when she saw me anyway.

I placed a finger to my lips and pointed at Rachel. Ava seemed to understand.

"You should get some sleep too," she whispered, stepping into the room and coming quietly up behind me.

I shook my head. "I promised Rachel I'd watch him."

Ava knelt down to look at Gabe. I turned to look at her as she shook her head slowly.

"Dammit…" she whispered under her breath, pressing her fingers to her lips. She didn't say anything else. She gently stroked Gabe's head for a moment.

"You think there's anything we can do?" I whispered, looking from Ava to the dog. "Do you think he'll…"

I didn't finish. I didn't have to.

Dabbing her eyes with the back of her hand, Ava shook her head. She got to her feet, patting my shoulder gently as she stood.

"Make sure you get some sleep," she whispered again.

I nodded slowly. I listened to her leave; the door clicked quietly shut behind her.

Taking a deep breath, I leaned over the tiny mutt. He lay there stiffly for a moment before his chest finally swelled again with oxygen.

I breathed a little sigh of relief, sprawling out on my side next to him, propping myself up on my elbow. I gently brushed my fingertips across his scruffy head, scratching his ears.

"Sorry this happened to you, bud," I whispered softly. "You definitely didn't deserve it…"

I watched him draw another labored breath. This time he let out a little whimper as he exhaled. My heart sank a little; he sounded so pitiful.

"Shhh," I soothed, moving my fingers gently along his neck and down to his leg. "It's alright… I'm not going to hurt you, I promise."

I glanced over at Rachel, making sure she was still sleeping. Her hair draped over her face, and her mouth hung open as she drew deep, unconscious breaths.

I carefully moved my hands down along Gabe's body, stopping when I got to his leg. He lifted his head slightly only to lower it again, too weak to hold it up.

"Shhh," I hushed again, carefully working on the bandage, unwinding it from the dog's tiny leg.

Carefully peeling away the blood-splotched layers, I started to assess how much damage had actually been done. The flesh on Gabe's leg was bloodied with deep lacerations from the teeth of the dog that had attacked him. His leg was an absolute wreck, and I was guessing the bone was broken. God knows how much blood he'd already lost.

Ava was right: this would be a major, expensive vet visit—if they were even capable of saving him at all.

I heaved a sigh, turning to look over at Rachel. She hadn't stirred.

My gaze trailed back to Gabe as he panted another weak breath. With the bandage off now, blood began to drizzle from his leg wound.

"Shit…"

I quickly slid my hand under his wounded front leg, cupping it gently and reaching for the bloodied bandage to wrap it up again. Warm droplets of blood trickled to my hand as I looped the bandage around his paw and began to gently bind his leg, my fingertips brushing his mangled flesh as I wrapped it—or at least attempted to. My hands started shaking.

Stopping for a moment, I dropped the rest of the bandage to glance down at my trembling fingers. For a moment I just stared, my mind flashing back to that morning—reaching for the pencil and watching it drift away from my fingertips.

Did I just imagine it lifting from the floor?

I flexed my fingers, attempting to steady my breath. Fixing my eyes on Gabe, I picked up the slack bandage and started to wrap his leg again. Then I stopped. I squinted, examining the wound more closely. Somehow, it looked different than it had only moments ago.

I couldn't quite grasp why, but then, as I leaned closer, I began to notice that it was no longer bleeding. The dog took a whining breath and lifted his muzzle slightly before setting it back down again. I placed one hand on his head, stroking my trembling fingers reassuringly over his bristly fur. To my surprise, he instantly calmed.

I swallowed hard, looking back down at the wound. I studied it again—the gash that had stained my fingertips red only moments ago was *no longer bleeding*.

Carefully, I cupped my hand beneath the dog's paw once more, my fingers gently making contact with his mangled flesh. A burning sensation sizzled through my fingertips. Jerking back, I looked down at my hands, my eyes wide. I expected to see a burn mark.

Everything looked normal.

I closed my eyes for a moment, breathing heavily as a wave of dizziness came over me. I looked back down at Gabe but caught only blurs of his tiny body, his half-bandaged leg. Reaching out, I gently grasped his paw, trying to focus—trying to blink away the dizzy, swirling mess the room and everything in it had become, but to no avail. Everything swayed and collapsed into darkness.

I dropped to the floor.

"What is it you like about running?" I heard a muffled voice say.

I could just make out Ms. Wu's face in front of me, but her features were blurry and smudged, like someone had tried to erase them. My eyes felt out of focus, my body as heavy as lead.

"I like being outside," I heard my voice reply, faint and distorted. "Climbing things… jumping over obstacles… You know, like parkour."

Each word rolled off my tongue and crashed to the floor, heavy and sinking like I felt.

"And what is it you like about parkour?" Ms. Wu asked, the pitch of her voice bending and curving, interrupted by blips of what sounded like TV static.

"I guess I like the way it makes me feel."

More static. "How's that?"

"Fast…" The word slowed and stretched. "Free."

For a moment my focused flickered in and out; then it finally cleared around Ms. Wu's face. Except her face looked different than normal; she wasn't smiling, and her eyes were dark and clouded with something heavy.

"No, Ion," she replied at last, slowly shaking her head. "You will never be free…"

I stared at her, wanting to ask why, wanting to say something, but finding I could do little more than focus on the blurry features of her face—her dark eyes.

"You can never be free because of where you come from…" Her words twisted through the air and hit me like knives. "Because of who you are…"

The floor seemed to suck me in deeper, pulling me farther and farther down into the murky substance that it was becoming until I was craning my neck to stare up at the blurry, distorted version of my math teacher.

"Because you're an anomaly, Ion…" Her whispered voice slowed like freezing water. "You can run as fast… and as far as you can… but you will never… never be free…"

The words rattled through my skull like a migraine.

Anomaly.

The very word turned my stomach. It seemed to collapse on me like a tidal wave, rushing over my head and filling my lungs every time I reached for a breath. I couldn't *breathe…*

I could feel cold swirling water around my feet. I glanced down to find icy-blue lake water splashing up around my ankles. The burning sensation in my hands was a stark contrast to the frozen sensation filling my insides as I slowly lifted my gaze to find the lake stretched out in front of me.

A chaos of words echoed inside me, voices that shouted over each other, tearing my mind apart like demons.

You're a piece of garbage, Ion… No one wants you…

What if I just disappeared? Would anyone notice?

I stared out at the lake, unable to feel my body now; all I could feel was the cold.

Would anyone care?

The lake wasn't blue anymore; it wasn't sparkling with sunlight anymore. No, on the horizon dark gray clouds were creeping forward, stretching over the opaque water like ash stains. The wind rippled across the surface and ruffled my dark hair, seeming to whisper for me to come closer—seeming to reiterate my question:

Would anyone care?

I closed my eyes and took a deep breath, starting to step forward—

"Ion, wait!"

A voice caught me before I could move any farther. I whipped around to look in the direction the voice had come from, but as soon as I moved, my head spun and everything blurred around me, crashing again into a familiar darkness.

I took a breath for what felt like the first time in a while. For a moment I felt completely lost and disoriented. Then, slowly, I became aware of carpet underneath me.

I lay there for a moment, stiff and hardly able to move. I tried to collect my thoughts and recall where I was and what had happened to me before I'd gone unconscious, but I could remember nothing.

I slowly peeled one eye open, only to squeeze it tightly shut again as blinding white light slapped across my face. I grumbled and rolled over, planting my face into the thick carpet. My limps were numb and prickling. Something warm grazed my ear.

I flicked it away with my hand.

The warm, wet something touched my ear again.

Groaning, I brushed it away again, rolling over onto my back to draw a deeper breath—and something suddenly pounced on my rib cage, knocking the breath out of me.

Startled and coughing, I opened my eyes. It took a moment of blinking and squinting for them to adjust to the bright light filling the room, but when they did, they focused immediately on the small scruffy outline looming just above my face, tongue out, drizzling drool onto my cheeks.

SIX

FOR A MOMENT I just lay there on the carpet and stared up at the grinning dog on top of me, my eyes wide and my heart pounding in my throat. An unraveled bandage trailed from his leg, which now looked completely normal. No gash, no blood, just clean, fur-covered flesh.

Gabe tilted his head, staring down at me for a moment before diving forward to lather my face with his saliva.

Snapping out of my stupefied daze, I bolted upright, sending the dog scampering to the floor as I crawled feverishly backward. My back hit the wall, knocking the air out of me. I sat there for a moment staring down at the scruffy gray mop of fur. He stared back at me, panting and letting his long pink tongue drape over his jaw like a banner.

I scrambled to my feet, back still pressed to the wall.

How… the hell…?

Gripping a handful of my hair, I shot a glance at Rachel. She was still curled up in bed, sound asleep.

I looked back down at Gabe just as he surged forward to jump up and plant his two front paws on my knees. For a moment I stood frozen—stunned.

Then I bolted.

Jolting away and leaping over the mutt, I sprinted out of the room, opening the door just enough to slip back out into the hallway before quickly closing it again behind me. Immediately I heard the quiet thud of Gabe's paws on the other side, followed by obsessive scratching. I leaned back, bracing my arms against it, breathing like I'd just finished running a marathon.

My mind reeled back to the night before—to after Rachel had fallen asleep and I'd sat on the floor next to Gabe. I started to remember how I'd unwound the bandage from his leg to check to see if it was broken. I could still remember how it had looked: the mauled, bloodied flesh.

Now it looked fine.

How?

How?

How the hell?

I massaged my eye sockets with the heels of my hands; then slowly I pulled them away from my face to gape down at them. They were still splotched with dried mutt blood from when my fingers had brushed the wound, when my hands had started to tremble and burn.

My hands…

I studied my palms. They didn't shake or feel like they were ablaze now—they felt completely normal, like they should.

I kept wishing I could convince myself that I was imagining things: the hovering pencil, the punch, and now the dog. Oh, God,

I wished I could just wake up to find that this whole thing had been nothing more than a long, tiring nightmare.

I heard the stirring of sleepy morning sounds in the kitchen: cabinets creaking open, footsteps, water being poured.

I took a deep breath, stepping away from the door to walk to a window at the end of the hallway whose blinds were still drawn. I pulled down a few blades and peered out to the driveway. The pickup truck was still absent.

Sucking in a breath, I turned and walked into the kitchen. Ava was leaning against the counter at the other side of the room, wearing pajama pants and a baggy sweatshirt. She massaged her temples, her eyes squeezed shut. The coffee maker gurgled, streaming hot black liquid into the pot below. She didn't look up when I walked in.

I tried to be silent as I skirted the kitchen table, attempting to make an escape for the stairs. But there was no sneaking past Ava.

"Ion."

A sigh caught in my throat as my shoulders fell. I turned slowly to face her. "Yeah?"

She was still leaning against the counter, but her eyes weren't closed anymore. They were locked with mine; one dark eyebrow was raised.

"We need to talk," she said; she sounded fatigued, resigned.

I stood there for a moment before stepping back into the kitchen, forcing one foot in front of the other. Ava tipped her head toward one of the kitchen chairs.

I pulled it out and sat down. Ava pulled out the chair across from me and sat down.

"How's Gabe doing?" she asked.

I swallowed, not sure what to say, but thankfully Ava took my prolonged hesitation as a bad sign and went on before I could answer.

"I really appreciate you staying with Rachel last night," she said quietly. "It means a lot…"

I rubbed my hands over my thighs, racking my brain for something to say.

"Look at me, please, Ion."

I ran a hand back through my messy hair; my tired eyes met her probing ones as she leaned forward a little, clearing her throat and taking on a new, more serious tone.

"Michael said he punched you in the face at school yesterday because you attacked him," she began. "Is that true?"

My voice thickened in my throat as I contemplated my reply. As if on cue, I heard the shower turn on upstairs. Michael was up, getting ready for school.

She perked a dark eyebrow questioningly, and finally I leaned a little closer.

"If Michael had punched me in the face, don't you think I'd look a little worse for wear?" I asked carefully.

Ava's expression didn't shift. "What actually happened, then? I saw Michael's bruises."

I shrugged. "Michael picks a lot of fights—how am I supposed to know who it was this time?"

"Michael said it was *you*."

"Michael's wanted to see the back of me since the moment I stepped through the door," I replied, leveling with her. "You and I both know that."

Ava sighed, dragging a hand over her face. She got up and walked over to the counter. "You have to try to get along with Michael, Ion—he's Mike's son. If you can't make it work…"

She didn't have to finish. I already knew the answer. I would go back to the agency, and the Reeveses would resume their normal, chaotic life sans a teenage boy who was losing his mind.

"I understand." I bobbed my head in a nod.

What a lie that was; I didn't understand anything. I was fricking terrified. Actually, I was only sitting there talking to her to keep my mind occupied—to keep myself from running all the way back to the lake and this time diving in headfirst. God, this was all so crazy…

"Coffee?" she asked, just as a high-pitched squeal interrupted the quiet. It only took a second to identify the voice.

Rachel.

Ava immediately set the pot down and strode out of the kitchen. I heard her footsteps quicken as she made her way down the hall toward Rachel's bedroom.

Pushing back my chair, I crossed the room and stopped at the counter, taking the pot out of the coffee maker and pouring myself a large mug of the steamy black liquid. I didn't even care that it burned my throat; I drained it in a few gulps.

I could hear Ava's voice mixed with Rachel's excited screeches and Gabe's incessant yelping. Unable to stand there listening any longer, I made a mad dash for the stairs, taking them two at a time. The bathroom door was still shut tight, and steam was seeping out through the crack under it. I stepped into my room and closed the door behind me, locking it.

As soon as I turned to face the desk across the room, I noticed the pencil lying on the floor. My jaw set, I strode across the room and bent down to snatch the pencil off the floor, gripping it tightly in my fist. I stared down at it for a moment, hot anger flooding my veins.

You are normal—you have to be.

In one quick motion I snapped the pencil in half and hurled it across the room. I threw myself down into my desk chair, grabbing the homework assignment Ms. Wu had given me the day before.

Pre-algebra. As if I didn't already hate my life enough as it was.

Massaging my head in my hands, I took a deep breath and stared down at the assignment for a solid minute, my mind drifting, before I forced myself to focus on the first problem. God, it all looked like such gibberish; I felt like I was suffocating, trying to get my mind to train itself on the black and white squiggles in front of me.

I reached for a pencil, but my fingers groped at the empty desk.

Right. I only had that one.

Gritting my teeth and muttering curses, I threw back my chair and got to my feet, reluctantly turning to scan the floor to see where I'd sent the two halves of the pencil scattering to.

But they weren't on the floor. Instead they hung, static and suspended for a moment before slowly, as if brushed by an invisible and unfelt breeze, tumbling in midair—rolling through the atmosphere, edging closer and closer.

My stomach bottomed out.

No... no, no, no, no, no...

One half of the pencil dipped through the air and came to hover over the desk. The other half drifted in the opposite direction.

Sweat beaded at the back of my neck as I dodged for the door. Twisting the knob, I flung it open. I darted out into the hallway and slammed it shut behind me; the bathroom door farther down the hall opened at the exact same moment.

Michael ran his fingers through his damp hair, slouching in the cloud of steam pouring out from behind him. His eyes narrowed to slits as soon as he noticed me standing there, his lips twisting into a sneer of contempt. "What the hell are you doing?"

I forced myself to step away from the door, wiping away the sweat that was dripping off my forehead. "Nothing."

"What's in there?" He tried to peer past me at my bedroom door.

My throat tightened as Michael narrowed his eyes, trying to decipher me. "Nothing," I croaked.

He glowered only a moment longer before striding forward, shoving me out of the way, grabbing the doorknob and twisting it before I could protest. He flung it open so hard the knob bashed into the wall. I swallowed, almost afraid to turn around.

Michael turned to look at me, his eyes still narrow and suspicious. I looked at him for a moment before stealing a glance into the room's interior; my heart was beating so loud I was afraid he could hear it.

The room was still and quiet. The trees swayed outside the window. And two halves of a pencil lay static on the floor in the middle of the room.

Michael stepped closer to me, getting in my face and snapping me out of my terrified daze.

"My dad thinks I'm a coward, Ion," he hissed, his eyes drilling into mine. "He thinks I lied to him about decking you in the face. He thinks I don't know how to defend myself—even when my attacker is some scrawny little asshole like you." His eyes widened as he stared at me, sucking in a trembling breath. "But you and I both know what happened, Ion... I don't know how the hell you fixed your piece-of-shit face, but you and I both know exactly what happened..."

He slammed his hands into my chest, sending me stumbling backward a few feet. My trembling hands instantly heated up as I dragged my gaze back up to meet his. His lips folded into a sneer as he stepped closer.

"And if you think this is anywhere near over?" He shook his head slowly. "You're out of your mind."

SEVEN

I COULD BARELY KEEP my eyes open through class. The room seemed to flicker in and out of reality as my eyelids sank shut only to jolt open a moment later. I tried my best to focus, but it wasn't working for me, not after being up most of the night with the dog—the dog whose leg had definitely been broken. Yet, back at the Reeveses', he was bounding around Rachel's bedroom, barking up a storm, completely fine.

How?

It was the one word that kept vibrating in my mind like a penetrating drumbeat: *how, how, how?*

I couldn't stop thinking about it—all of it. That pencil floating in midair, spinning around the bedroom. The way I'd felt when my fingertips had brushed the dog's bloody wound; the strange vibration that had come into my hands along with that burning heat.

Why is this happening to me?

It had all seemingly begun when I'd been sitting at my desk, listening to Rachel go ballistic over her wounded dog. I could still see the gray sky beyond the window, and the dark mangled tree branches swirling against it. I felt like I was still sitting at that desk, reliving that moment every time I closed my eyes. That last moment of everything being normal.

But then… when have I ever really been normal?

"Ion, how about you answer this one?"

Ms. Wu's voice swam through the crackling static distortions of my mind to reach my long-lost attention. I only had to stare at her for a moment before she sighed and pointed to someone else. She kept me after class again, and this time her expression was a little less hopeful.

"Ion, you don't pay attention in class, you don't turn in your homework assignments, you don't take school seriously." Her words were weary, but undebatable; all true. "This has to stop."

"I tried to do the assignment you gave me," I explained.

"And?" Ms. Wu raised one dark eyebrow. "Where is it?"

I'd forgotten it on the desk. Michael had finally shoved past me and stormed downstairs to see what all the commotion was about, and I'd taken the opportunity to bolt back into my room and escape out my bedroom window and onto the porch roof before Ava came upstairs to look for me and ask me about the dog. I couldn't answer any of her questions; I needed time to come up with a cover story.

"I went for a run this morning and lost track of time," I answered.

"Why didn't you do the assignment last night?"

I bit my lip, rendering a shrug after a moment. "Sorry."

Ms. Wu studied me hard for a moment, then simply heaved a sigh. "I'm the one who's sorry. I wish I could just get you to focus in class…" She trailed off, looking down at the papers in front of her. "Is anything going on at home that's bothering you?"

"Nah, nothing like that."

Ms. Wu nodded slowly. "Try to do better on this next assignment, alright?"

"Yes, ma'am."

She gave me a stiff, conversation-over kind of nod. It was hard not to remember the strange, warped version of her I'd dreamed about the night before as I turned and walked out of the classroom.

What I'd wanted to tell Ms. Wu was that the trees taught me more than school. Being alone in the woods, or down by the lake—it made something in my middle hum. The things I learned in school—those felt more like someone had stuck a vacuum hose in my head and sucked away everything that mattered, leaving me empty and echoing.

The rest of the day passed like train cars at a railroad crossing: slow and seemingly without end. Michael made eye contact with me once, but I couldn't read his expression.

By the time school finally got out, I felt hollow and ready to go back to bed. Slinging my backpack over my shoulder, I pushed through the double doors and emerged into the sunlight and fresh air. I sucked it down into my lungs like I hadn't breathed all day. The scent of melted snow and thawing mud replaced the stench of cleaning products and stale air. I stood there for a moment, drinking it in, before resuming my brisk pace across the cement, walking past the corner of the building.

I got only a step farther before a set of sneakers stepped into view. Gritting my teeth, I lifted my gaze to find Michael standing there, rolling a joint. He squinted at me when I stopped, his eyes narrowing.

"You want to explain how you did it?" His question came out like a command. "Or will I have to pound it out of you?"

I squinted at him. "Explain what, exactly?"

"Oh, I don't know…" He trailed off, refocusing on what he was doing. "Before I got on the bus, I heard Rachel blabbering on about that stupid dog of hers," he said, and grunted. "Said you 'did magic' on his leg and that it's all better now. You want to explain what the hell that means?"

I brushed the question off. "No clue what you're talking about."

"Bullshit. You slept in Rachel's room last night with the dog," he shot back bluntly, pinching the joint between his teeth and taking a lighter out of his pocket. "Ava told me all about it, and I heard every word—she said that Gabe's leg was busted last night, but this morning…" He sheltered the small flame with his cupped hand as he brought the lighter to his lips. "This morning he was jumping around on her bed, barking—totally normal."

"You're bullshitting me." I feigned surprise.

"You know I'm not," he muttered. "You did something."

I gulped air, not responding, which only seemed to prove his point.

"Look, fine—I slept on the floor with the dog in Rachel's room so she would go to bed, alright?" I finally retorted. "She was freaking out—she didn't want to take her eyes off Gabe, so I told her I would watch him."

"Uh-huh. What did you do to him? Voodoo?"

"Nothing," I replied through gritted teeth. "I did *nothing*. The dog looked the same when I woke up. Maybe he just wasn't as bad off as we thought."

"He was beat to shit; I saw it with my own eyes." He took a long drag and stepped closer, smoke seeping past his lips. "You did something to that dog. Tell me what you did, or I'm going to tell my dad everything."

"Everything?" I reiterated, my voice coming out stiff. "Everything as in *what*, exactly? I haven't done anything to you—why can't you just leave me the hell alone?"

"I could have said the same thing to you when you punched me in the face, Ion—then lied to my dad about it." His expression hardened to steel as his cold eyes scanned my face. "You made my dad look at me like I was a coward, and I'm never going to let that happen again—ever."

"If your dad looks at you differently, that's your own fault," I snapped, taking a step closer. "You want to blame someone for that? Maybe you should look in the mirror."

With that, I brushed past him. Students were flowing out of the school and onto the walkway, forcing him to retreat back behind the building where no one would see him, but I could feel the burn of his gaze as I walked away.

I didn't want to go home—not yet. I didn't want to be interrogated about the dog; I didn't want to feel reality slip through my fingers. I wanted to hold onto the normal world for a little longer. I skipped the bus.

Maybe Michael was right. Maybe I shouldn't have punched him—maybe I should have just walked away from the fight. Maybe he had reason to be angry with me, to resent the fact that I'd made him look like a coward in front of his dad.

I kicked a stone on the sidewalk as I strode forward, keeping my eyes down.

My fingers trembled a little as I clenched the strap of my backpack. My head felt like it was spinning out of control. I felt sick—terrified—as the same tired questions sliced through my thoughts like knives. *What is wrong with me?*

I couldn't help but wonder if I should tell someone about what was happening to me… but who? There wasn't a human being in the world whom I trusted.

I picked up my pace to a jog, following the same route through town. I peeled off when I reached the turn for the state park, slowing up when I reached the familiar dirt road. The stiff spring breeze raked the barren branches of the trees, causing them to sway.

Cutting through the patch of woods, I emerged on the beach. I felt like today was just a replay of yesterday. Everything was happening the same way, but weirder. The only difference was that I hadn't punched anybody—yet.

I sat down on the cold sand, my back to a big weathered log the lake had spit out onto the beach, then slipped off my backpack and flipped it open to take out my math assignments and a pencil. I scanned over the same gibberish from the day before. Or maybe this gibberish was different—I wasn't sure. It all seemed to blend together, the lapping of the waves at the edge of the shore taking precedence in my mind.

Focus… Just stop thinking about everything but this…

It was so much easier said than done, but, gripping the pencil between my finger and thumb, I sorted through it as best I could. The inside of my head felt like it was on fire and I was barely halfway through.

Why was this important? Why did we have to spend so much time studying squiggles on a page when there were trees and lakes and wind that smelled like melting snow? The second seemed to light my senses on fire, whereas the first seemed only to dull them, smothering the faint beginnings of a spark inside my soul.

I watched the pencil tremble and shake in my grasp, flicking back and forth until it slipped out from between my fingers and dropped to the sand. I clenched my jaw as I squeezed my hands into fists, then spread them wide again.

Squinting out at the horizon, I saw the same hawk swooping and diving over the ruffled water. My eyes traced its wings spread like sails to catch the wind.

It could go wherever it wanted and no one could stop it. It could fly away from anything that tried to trap it or hold it back. That was the epitome of freedom—that hawk had everything I craved. Meanwhile, I was confined to squiggles on a page and a life of being an eraser smudge.

The more I thought about it, the more the vise inside me seemed to tighten, the more my hands seemed to shake.

I shoved the homework back into my backpack, hesitating a little before I picked up the pencil and tossed it into my backpack along with everything else.

I was about to get up and leave when a smudge in the distance caught my eye. I paused for a moment, then rose to my feet, shielding my eyes with my hand.

Being a sunny day, there were a handful of people on the beach, mostly older folks with oversized sunglasses and bundled up enough for an Arctic expedition. But someone in particular had caught my eye—a smudgy shape with a bundle of driftwood in his arm. It was the same old guy from the day before, wearing the same sweatshirt and beat-up ball cap.

For a moment I just stood there and watched, shouldering my backpack and flexing my trembling fingers. My eyes followed the old guy as he made his way farther and farther down the beach.

That same question resurfaced in my mind: *Should I tell someone?*

But this old guy didn't even know where I was from, or what my name was. He didn't know about the strange circumstances under which I'd been found. He didn't know *anything* about me…

My eyes drifted down to my hands and then back up to him as he moved steadily down the beach, picking up driftwood.

Perfect.

EIGHT

THE OLD MAN SQUINTED his eyes and turned my hand over to examine my palm, spreading my shaky fingers. I studied his face anxiously from where I sat across from him, seated on one of the old logs outside his driftwood hut. I felt rude, staring at him like that, but I couldn't help it.

"Flex your fingers," he said eventually.

I did as he asked, and he watched, bobbing his head in a slow nod. Leaning over, he picked a rock up off the sand and placed it in the center of my hand.

"Squeeze it."

I clenched my fist, but the muscles in my hand only weakened and gave way. The small smooth rock slipped easily out of my grasp and fell to the ground. I cursed, dragging my other hand over my face.

The old man sat back on the log across from mine, then picked up a piece of wood to gently place it on the kindling fire.

"You nervous about school lately?" he asked.

I considered it, my eyes following the golden sparks up into the sky. "I don't think a lot about school, to be honest." I sighed.

"Maybe if I was a little more nervous about it, I wouldn't be failing in so many things."

"What do you think you're failing in?"

"Math mostly," I replied, rubbing my forehead. "Some other stuff. I don't know. I just have a hard time focusing. My mind goes everywhere… I feel like there's something restless inside me that just won't stop…" I trailed off, running a hand through my hair. "I feel like everything is crumbling around me—I have questions about everything, even the things everyone else just accepts."

He pulled a package of what looked like granola out of the satchel on the ground next to him and threw it at me.

"Here," he muttered. "Maybe your blood sugar is low."

"Screw blood sugar," I groaned. "Have you ever felt like that?"

The old guy looked at me for a solid moment, squinting his eyes. Then he dipped his head in a single nod.

"Anyone who's awake questions," he said. "It's in our nature. To wrestle and fight—press everything we know and see how well it holds up." He started prodding the fire with a long stick. "We're not meant to be spoon-fed someone else's truth and forced to swallow."

"Someone else's truth?" I asked. "What do you mean by that?"

"I mean that truth is subject to interpretation. Everyone sees it differently—through their own lens, sprayed with the mud of their life," he said, keeping his eyes fixed on the fire. "Truth becomes like water, clouded by our pasts and our experiences. We only ever really know what's true when we're children, before the mud clouds our water. Before everyone tells us what and who we are."

I heaved a deep breath and leaned forward to rest my elbows on my knees. "No one's ever told me what or who I am, though. I've never known what the hell to believe about myself or who I am…"

I spread one hand and looked down at it. "Except a fluke in the system."

To my surprise, the old man laughed. "Good. We could use more flukes—the system is overrated."

I glanced up at him, confused. "You really *are* a hippie."

"We have too much vocabulary to associate with," he said, brushing off my accusation. "I'm simply someone who seeks the truth."

I stared at him for a moment longer. Then I ripped open the bag of granola.

I'd never heard anyone talk like this guy. He was as weird as they came, but I liked it. It was better than the normal stuff I heard every day at school. It was better than the voices I heard in my head—voices that were just ghosts of other people's words, telling me I was an eraser smudge.

"Try cutting caffeine out of your diet," he said.

I couldn't help but laugh. "No, no, that's not it."

"No?"

I shook my head. *Fairly certain caffeine can't make pencils float,* I thought but didn't say.

"I don't know how to describe it," I began slowly. "But ever since yesterday… I've just felt strange: like I'm out of control."

"We're never out of control," the old man replied, grabbing another log to toss into the flames. "Even when it feels like the whole world is spinning out of control, we're still masters of our own minds—we can control *that.*"

"Sometimes my mind feels like a runaway freight train."

"What we feel can often deceive."

I looked at him for a moment without answering.

What I felt…

Was I really in control of whatever was happening to me? It came and went like a tidal wave—and I felt just as incapable of stopping it from breaking. I felt like a mere spectator, watching my own mind grow teeth and claws to devour me with. In fact, every time the shaking started—that was when I started to let my mind go. When I would start to feel the warmth of anger swelling inside me, or the cold sting of sorrow, or the sear of self-conscious insecurity.

Like when Michael had stolen my homework and I'd missed the bus.

Like when he'd called me garbage.

It was the kind of feeling I would have imagined possession to feel like—it was like another person crawled into my skin and took over. Who was that person? I had no clue… and maybe I didn't have a say over how they acted. But maybe I could prevent the demons from creeping in; maybe I could barricade the door before they got there.

Maybe they snuck in all dressed up as feelings.

"That's when it happens…" I exhaled the words, my eyes going wide.

"What's that?"

I blinked back into focus, barely noticing that I'd spoken aloud. The old man's eyes were steady and intent as he stared at me from across the flames.

"Nothing," I responded after a moment. "Nothing."

Getting to my feet, I handed him back the bag of granola.

"Thanks for talking to me." I spoke the words like they were more of an apology than a thank you. "I gotta get back to the house now."

He bobbed his head in acknowledgment. "Take care of your-self."

I was so lost in thought I forgot to tell him to do the same. I forgot to ask him what his name was. Again.

My feet made scuffs in the sand as I walked, and the wind whipped my hair, freezing my skin and raising the hairs on the back of my neck. I shivered into my worn-out hoodie, pulling the hood up over my head. I paused when I reached the trees, looking back out at the lake, at the cold, lapping waves and the swooping, gliding hawk.

Maybe I could stop it. Maybe I could *make it stop…*

If I stopped *feeling.*

NINE

How to control your emotions...
How to maintain a positive mindset...
How to... not feel...

IT WAS 3:00 A.M. and my eyes were starting to burn from staring at the screen of my phone. I had school that day, regrettably, and I was going to feel like absolute shit, but I couldn't go to sleep. Not yet, not until I had found a scrap of an answer. Articles flicked past, and I scanned the subtitles. I stopped scrolling as I read the last title, my interest piqued. I clicked on it—a step-by-step WikiHow on how to be emotionally numb, with pictures. I grunted a mirthless laugh. This *had* to be a new all-time low.

I refocused on the screen, scrolling.

"Sometimes strong emotions can make it difficult for you to function, and you have to numb yourself temporarily just to get through the day..." I muttered, reading aloud. "Blah, blah, blah... Studies show that repressing negative emotions can deplete your psychological resources, making it more difficult for you to handle stress and make good decisions... Yeah, sure. Whatever..."

Most of it was fluffy bullshit. I skipped farther down the page.

"Control your environment… avoid people, events, and places you don't like." I rubbed a hand over my face. "Easier said than done… exercise… mute your emotions during stressful situations…"

I read through the rest.

"Keep a diary… Hmm…" I pinched my lower lip absent-mindedly between my forefinger and thumb, leaning closer to the screen. "Expel your emotions by writing them down in a journal. This will allow you to forget about your emotional state and move on with your life."

Move on with your life. Those five words seemed to leap off the screen to grab me by the throat.

It was like a mantra of everything I'd wanted to do for as long as I could remember—finally, *finally* shed the tired, old skin of my past and leave it in the dust. All the strange looks and hesitant questions, all the pushing and shoving and changing schools and "families," only for the same vicious cycle to repeat again and again.

I was intrigued and willing to give it a shot, even though part of me felt a little ridiculous when I pulled the composition notebook out of my backpack.

Oh, come on. What harm could it possibly do?

I flipped to a fresh page unmarred by bleary schoolwork scribblings. I grabbed a pencil and took a steady sip of air.

Yesterday I punched Michael Reeves in the face and felt good about doing it. Maybe that's wrong, I don't know, but even though I felt shitty about it afterward because of the trouble it caused, it felt kind of nice to defend myself for once. To feel like I could actually hold my own.

But it also scared me. Not so much because of the action itself, but because of how I felt like I couldn't control what I did—I felt like I couldn't hold back the pure frickin' rage I felt inside me. Is it normal to get so angry? I wish I could ask someone about it.

I paused, glancing down at the pencil in my hand; a sinking feeling settled in my gut as my mind flashed back to the horror show the morning had been. The entire day had quickly followed suit, except for my conversation with the old man.

When I'd gotten home, Rachel had tackled me, squealing, "Thank you, thank you, thank you!" in deafening repetition. I'd had to act like a dick and tell her to get off me—that I had no clue what she was talking about, because Mr. Reeves was sitting right there in the living room, watching TV and drinking his booze. He hadn't said anything to me; he'd just shot me a dirty look, the kind I knew well. The kind that spelled out *I wish you weren't here.*

It was nothing compared to when Ava got home from work, though. She'd made me sit down at the kitchen table and tried to pry answers out of me. She'd prefaced the whole thing with a stern, "Never climb out onto the roof again. It's dangerous; do you understand me?"

Yes, I understood—that was what I'd told her. What she didn't understand was that potentially taking a tumble from the rooftop was the least of my concerns.

"Ion, Rachel told me you healed Gabe's wounded leg," she'd begun, her voice weighed down with concern. "Did you?"

I shook my head without hesitation.

"Ion, I want you to think about it before you answer, alright?"

"I already answered—I didn't do anything, I swear." My voice came out strained. "Like I told you, when you came in to check on Rachel, she asked me to stay up and watch the dog. She was exhausted, and you guys were…" I hesitated, clearing my throat. "You and Mr. Reeves were having an argument. So I thought it might… help her if I stayed and watched the dog so she could sleep."

Ava's eyes softened a little, her lips pressing into a sad smile. "That was very considerate of you, Ion."

I just shrugged.

"So you have no idea what happened to Gabe?"

I shook my head again, even more adamantly this time. "No idea. I was just as surprised as Rachel was."

Ava had just looked at me and nodded slowly. "If it was such a surprise to you, Ion, why didn't you tell me about it when you came into the kitchen this morning?"

My lips parted with a messy response that trailed off to nothing, leaving us to just sit there in uncomfortable silence for a moment before Mr. Reeves lumbered into the room and started bitching about something. I couldn't even remember what he'd said, but I could still see Ava's dark, piercing eyes studying me like I was a complicated math problem. I could feel her pain—I was even more dazed and confused.

I shoved the day out of my thoughts, trying to forget about it and focus on the matter at hand, dropping my focus back down to the page of messy pencil scratches. I added a few more lines to the chaos.

Damn it, I wish pencils would just stop floating. Why did that have to happen?

The last six words looked so haunted, it scared me. I almost wished I hadn't done this—written it down.

The worst part is that I can't tell anyone. Not even the old guy at the beach. He wouldn't have talked to me if he'd known about the things I've done—no one would.

I closed the composition notebook and clicked off the light before I had a chance to look at the pencil, or even think about it.

————————

I woke up with the dawn. I felt like I'd barely slept, and when I had, it was only for short periods of time; the inconsistent waves of unconsciousness had been murky with nightmare debris. My eyes were bleary with exhaustion as I descended the staircase. I stepped into the living room to discover that I was the first one up. Mr. Reeves was passed out on the couch in the living room, and the early gray light was filtering through the blinds.

I walked softly into the kitchen and opened the blinds over the window above the kitchen sink. I squinted as the tired light cut through to burn my weary eyes. I raked my hands back through my tangled hair and stifled a yawn.

In the silence of the early morning, the old man's words seemed to reverberate:

"... truth is subject to interpretation... everyone sees it differently... we only ever really know what's true when we're children, before everyone tells us what and who we are..."

If everyone had their own truth, what was mine? Was it how I felt, or what I thought? The strange things that were happening to me, seemingly beyond my control... Were *they* the *truth*?

I swallowed the sick feeling lingering at the back of my throat, forcing myself to stop thinking about it—to stop feeling. I opened a cabinet and took out a can of coffee. I filled the pot with tap water and poured it into the reservoir of the coffee maker. I fished around until I found a filter; then I scooped some dirt out of the can.

I sat down at the kitchen table and rested my head in my hands. A warm, rich scent filled the room as the coffee began to brew.

I returned to the question that still haunted me: was this nightmare I was living the truth?

No. No, the weird shit that was tormenting me was not the truth—it was... I wasn't sure what it was exactly, but I wasn't about to give in to it.

It's just your emotions... That's all... Just don't feel.

I rehashed what I'd read the night before, going over the steps.

Mute your emotions...

avoid people and things and places that make you feel out of control...

control your environment...

control your thoughts....

Easy.

A sudden, soft *tick, tick, tick* filled the room. A moment later I felt two paws pressing against my leg.

Heaving a sigh, I glanced under the table. A pair of large soupy brown eyes stared back at me.

"Get lost, Gabe," I muttered, shooing him away. "You've screwed my life up enough as it is… No need to rub it in…"

The terrier mutt was persistent as hell. He put his paws back up on my legs. I brushed him away. Again with the paws.

"Stop," I hissed firmly. This time his ears folded back and he stepped away for a second.

"How can you be mean to Gabe?" a new, small voice said behind me.

I jerked around in my chair. Rachel stood in the doorway, dressed in a fleece PJ onesie. Her scraggly blond hair hung down over her shoulders and her blue eyes were half awake. She stared at me like an owl, and I quickly placed a finger to my lips.

"Shhh. Your dad's sleeping," I whispered.

Rubbing her eyes with her small fists, she padded over and stopped at my chair. She yawned and leaned her head against my shoulder. "Ion."

She said nothing else. I could tell she was waiting for me to ask "What?"

I sucked in a tired breath. "What, Rachel?"

"How come you told them you didn't do it?" she asked quietly.

"Do what?"

"Make Gabe better."

"Because I didn't." I gently placed a hand on her shoulder to push her to arm's distance, looking her right in the eyes. "I didn't do anything to Gabe, Rachel. You gotta stop talking like that, alright?"

Her lips turned into a stubborn frown. "But I saw you."

I opened my mouth to speak, but then everything inside me froze.

"Wait—you what?"

"I woke up… I woke up just for a minute, and I saw you unwrapping his bandages," Rachel whispered, looking straight into my eyes. "I saw what happened."

I swallowed. "I was just checking on his leg."

Her messy blond hair rippled as she adamantly shook her head. "I saw what happened when you touched him, Ion. What happened to his wound—how it got better…"

Sweat prickled over the back of my neck. *Shit.*

The gears in my mind turned faster. I sucked in a breath to steady myself.

"Okay, okay." I lowered my voice. "I'm going to tell you something."

"How you healed Gabe?"

I nodded. "But first I need to know—did you tell anyone anything about what you saw?"

She nodded. "Momma."

"You told her everything you saw?"

She rocked back and forth on her bare feet, puffing her cheeks contemplatively. "Well, I didn't have a chance to tell her everything yet—she was running out the door, and then last night she said she was too tired." A smile tugged at her lips. She lowered her voice. "Tell me how you did it."

Relief flooded my veins. "Okay, look—I need you to promise me something first, okay?"

Her lips twitched into that same stubborn frown again. "What?"

"Promise me you won't tell anyone about what you saw—no one."

"How come?"

The gears in my head started turning. "Because… the, uh… the magic goes away if people know about it." I tried my best to sound serious. "Gabe's leg will go back to being broken if you tell anyone what I'm about to tell you."

Her big blue eyes went wide. "No!"

I pushed a finger against my lips again. "Shhhh. Quiet… If your dad wakes up, I won't be able to tell you anything."

She pursed her lips and sat down in the chair across from me, sitting on her folded legs. "Okay, okay," she whispered intently. "I promise. I won't even tell Momma."

I reached across the table and stuck out my pinky, giving her a hard look. She stared at me for a moment before grumbling a sigh and locking her little finger around my own.

"Now tell me." She sighed impatiently. "Tell me about the magic."

I took a deep breath and thought about it for a moment, resting my head on my fist.

"Well… years ago, when I was right around your age…" I trailed off, wondering how the hell I was going to end that sentence. I bit my lip and checked to see if she was paying attention.

She was. Hard-core.

"I lived with another family. They lived up in the mountains and kept me locked away in their barn with all the animals," I fibbed. "They made me work every single day, without food or water."

"Are you serious?" Her eyes were massive. "No food ever?"

"Okay, a bowl of rice and a cup of water once a day," I admitted. "But no more than that. Anyway, there was no way out—the door was always locked—"

"What about windows?"

"There was one of those—but the barn was right on the very edge of the cliff. If you climbed out the window, you would plummet, down, down, down—thousands of feet to a grisly death."

Her expression was intense. "So how did you escape?"

"Well, I was in the barn, right? So… there were chickens and ducks and stuff like that. Lots of those, actually. So at night when everyone was asleep, I started gathering up as many feathers as I could find. I saved them for weeks," I continued quietly but seriously. "One day I was able to steal a few long, skinny pieces of wood. I waited until I had gathered enough chicken and duck feathers, and then… one night…"

"What?"

I held her in suspense for a moment while I made up the rest, recalling the ancient Greek myth I was basing it on, something I'd read ages ago.

"One night I took some of the tools, and I nailed together some wood in the shape of wings and covered them with feathers," I went on. "I strapped them on, flung open the window, and leapt out into the darkness."

Rachel let out a little gasp. "Did you fall?"

I shook my head, grinning a little. She was eating it all up.

"I flew," I said. "I flew until dawn—until morning and then afternoon, when the sun rose high in the sky." I shot her a look. "But that's where I ran into trouble."

"Trouble?"

"The sun was so bright and beautiful—it felt so nice and warm as I flew over the rolling, green mountains. I just kept flying higher and higher." I closed my eyes. I could see the diving, swooping hawk flying over the surface of the lake behind my closed lids. "I felt so free… I just wanted to keep going and going and going…" My throat tightened a little as I trailed off.

"Then what happened?"

I took a steady breath. "The sun started to melt the glue, and all the feathers came flying off the wings I'd made, stripping them to sticks."

"Then you fell."

I thought about it for a second. I pictured myself playing the part of Icarus in the Greek myth; flapping my featherless popsicle sticks, knowing what was about to happen; realizing, as I hovered there in midair with the sun burning across my skin, that I was about to plummet to my death.

Then I fell…

I couldn't help but feel like there was something inside me that was taking over. Something was changing me. My feathers were fluttering to the ground, and I was stuck in midair, drenched in sweat, gasping for breath, screaming at the top of my lungs:

Please don't let me fall, please don't let me fall, please don't let me fall…

Then I fell… Was that the next line in my story? Was that my truth?

"Ion?"

Rachel's inquisitive tone snapped me back down to earth. I blinked and straightened back up.

"No, I didn't fall," I answered finally, my voice quiet. "The sun reached out and caught me in its hands. Its fire flooded through me—filling me with light. And that's how the magic came to me."

She stared at me, completely thunderstruck. "Because you were touched by the sun?"

I looked at her for a moment, then broke a little smile. I nodded. "Because I was touched by the sun."

TEN

THE NEXT DAY CAME and went: normal. I sat down at my desk that night and opened my composition notebook.

> I passed the math test.
> I didn't have any run-ins.
> Nothing floated.
> I didn't hurt anyone.
> A good day.

Saturday morning I slept in a little. I found Ava in the kitchen making breakfast when I went downstairs. Rachel was already sitting at the table, devouring a plate of eggs and pancakes. I peered around, expecting to see Mr. Reeves lumbering around in a beat-up tank top with a mug of spiked coffee in his hand.

Ava glanced at me over her shoulder. "Morning, Ion."

I stepped farther into the room. "Morning."

Rachel looked up when I spoke, smiling through full cheeks.

"Where's Mr. Reeves?" I asked cautiously.

Ava didn't respond for a moment, but when she finally did, she simply said, "Out."

I knew better than to ask more. I walked over to the coffee pot and poured myself some.

"I have to apologize, Ion," Ava said quietly. "For pressing you about Gabe and his... unreal recovery. Rachel told me she was just teasing about you healing his leg." She sighed a little, then smiled. "I thought she was serious and could think of no other reasonable explanation."

I slid the pot back into the coffee maker. "No need to apologize. It was a simple misunderstanding."

I shot Rachel a glance over the rim of my mug, and she gave me a wink. She still believed I was magical.

"Yes, but some misunderstandings haven't been so simple lately." She sighed again, turning back to the old stove. "And even though my husband won't say so, I'm sorry for that, too."

She was talking about Michael accusing me of punching him in the face. So she didn't believe I did it. I guess she'd bought my side of the story after all...

I swallowed back a little pang of guilt. By now I was getting used to killing even the faintest flicker of an emotion.

"No worries," I mumbled, draining the rest of the mug— wishing it were something stronger. Something that could numb me thoroughly and stop my mind from hissing out through my ears like steam.

"Pancakes?" she offered, lifting one from the pan with the spatula.

I said no, thanks, that I wasn't hungry, but she insisted. So I sat across from Rachel and ate breakfast with Gabe begging at my heels. Rachel didn't say much, but the looks she kept giving me were enough. I started to wish I hadn't made the story so elaborate... but then it *had* gotten me off the hook. Hell, it'd even thrown off Ava's suspicions about whether there was any validity to Michael's side of the story.

Life was better than it had been in a while.

Maybe it was a bad idea to rub in the fact that Ava trusted me, but after breakfast I went into the living room and threw myself down on the couch with a stack of homework assignments. Michael peeled his eyes away from the TV screen to shoot me a glare.

"What are you doing?" he spat.

I shrugged, looking down at the pages in my lap. "Homework."

"Do it somewhere where I don't have to look at you, then."

"Last time I checked, I live here too."

He grunted. "Temporarily, and hopefully not for much longer."

It bothered me, I'll admit it—but I quickly muted it along with the battle noises from the video game and focused on the page in front of me.

"I'll find a way to make sure you leave," he muttered after a moment, his eyes glued to the screen again. "Do you really think I'm going to just sit around and watch Ava talk my dad into believing that you didn't attack me—"

"You started it—"

"You threw the first punch," he sliced in icily. "And you're going to pay for it."

I rolled my eyes and looked back down at my work, gripping the pencil firmly.

"What the hell happened to your parents anyway?"

The abrupt question jarred me out of my thoughts; the muscles in my jaw tensed. For a moment I just stared at the page.

"I mean, like, did they both die or…?" He trailed off, biting his lip as he tilted back and forth, vigorously punching buttons on the controller. "Or did they just toss you in the dumpster after taking one look at you?"

The words cut like shrapnel, instantly summoning that warm, tight, sick feeling inside me—the feeling that always came right before the shaking did.

"I mean, not that I can blame them." Michael snorted a laugh. "But still, I'm kinda curious."

I pinned my gaze on the next math problem, forcing my mind to focus on the math and nothing else.

Don't feel, don't feel, don't feel.

I pushed the anger down, but it seemed to do nothing more than stoke the fire and intensify all the sounds around me. I redirected my thoughts—imagining myself ripping the gaming console out of the TV set and smashing it on the floor right in front of Michael. Or lighting it on fire.

It was almost as satisfying as punching him in the face—almost. But at least it could do no damage.

"Hello? Ion! I'm talking to you, moron—answer me," Michael's harassment was gathering strength. "Hey…"

I ignored him, venting my anger into a mental image of myself destroying Michael's favorite possession: the gaming console. The pencil trembled in my grasp.

"Hey, freakface!"

I was jolted out of my thoughts as pain surged through my head. I flinched backward as something small and hard struck me in the skull. "Look at me when I talk to you!"

The small black remote control Michael had thrown at me dropped into my lap. I slowly straightened up, looking back up at Michael.

His eyes were ablaze with anger as he stared back at me. Without a word, I collected my homework and stood. I walked slowly across the room and turned off the gaming console on my way out—just to piss him off.

Michael exploded into hateful curses.

"Michael Reeves!" Ava shouted, stepping into the living room. "That is no way to talk to someone..."

I didn't hear the rest. I was already pounding up the stairs, heading for my room. I slammed the door shut behind me and leaned back against it, breathing hard.

I held my hands out in front of me and looked down at my palms. My fingers were as shaky as if I'd just downed a few cans of Red Bull.

Shit, shit, shit...

Clenching my fists, I crossed the room and sat down at my desk. Flipping open my composition notebook, I turned to a fresh page and picked up the pencil lying beside it.

I feel nothing, I wrote.

I feel nothing,

I feel nothing,

I feel nothing.

I scrawled the same line over and over and over again, the handwriting even more spidery and trembling than normal.

Lies,

Lies,

Lies.

Finally I stopped, throwing the pencil down on the desk, burying my face in my hands. My throat tightened and my eyes swelled with tears.

"Why can't I stop… why can't I just stop?" My voice came out in a tired, mumbled whisper. "Why can't I just stop feeling?"

The longer I sat there, the more my hands trembled against my face, growing warmer and warmer until finally they were hot. I couldn't even touch my skin anymore: it burned.

I pushed back my chair and turned around. My stomach bottomed out.

My backpack, the dirty clothes I'd left on the floor, the crumpled blanket on the foot of my bed, my sneakers—they all hung suspended in midair. I swallowed, standing there, staring in disbelief.

Then someone knocked on the door, already beginning to open it at the same time.

"Ion?" Ava's voice.

My eyes widened and I bolted forward, throwing myself against the door. "One second—I'm dressing!"

"Sorry! Sorry, sorry," she apologized in machine-gun repetition. "I thought you had already gotten dressed…"

My eyes darted back and forth as I leaned back against the door. "I spilled something on my jeans."

I snatched the sneakers out of midair and shoved them under the bed along with my clothes. The backpack had already drifted all the way up to the ceiling and out of reach. I cursed under my breath.

"Okay, just let me know when I can come in."

I cursed some more. "Yeah—yeah, just a sec."

I dragged my desk chair over and climbed up onto it, reaching for the strap of my backpack, which was hovering just above me. My shaking fingers closed around it just as the chair beneath me began to shift, dumping me over onto the floor. Thankfully, the backpack was still in my hand.

"Ion? Ion, are you okay?"

I rolled over onto my back, scrambling onto my ass. The back legs of the chair were beginning to peel up off the floor. I threw myself onto it before it could begin to float.

"Ion?" Ava repeated, concerned now.

I cleared my throat, my head spinning. "Uh, yeah—yeah, I'm fine. Come in."

The door opened and Ava stepped in. I tried to ignore the anxiety swelling inside me as I sat there rigidly, clutching my backpack to my chest. I watched Ava's discerning blue eyes give the room a careful scan before they centered on me.

"What was that bang I heard in here?"

I raked my fingers back through my hair, leaning back in the chair. "Bang? Oh, oh… I, uh, I tripped."

One dark eyebrow perked. "You tripped?"

I nodded a little too adamantly.

"Aren't those the same jeans you were wearing before?" Ava asked, giving me a questioning once-over. "They look exactly the same."

I shook my head. "Similar but different," I fibbed.

She nodded slowly, seeming unconvinced.

"Did you need me for something?" I asked before she could question further.

"No, no, you're fine," she replied, pursing her lips. "I only came to apologize for the way Michael treated you downstairs just now. No one should ever have to endure being treated like that."

I shrugged. "I've been treated worse."

Ava's lips turned into a sad frown. "I wish there was something I could do to help you, Ion."

Her words were so sincere, it took me aback a little. I swallowed back a different kind of tightness in my throat and forced a little nod. "Ditto."

Ava looked equally taken aback as she stood there, staring back at me. Her thin, pursed lips wobbled a little; then she took a steady breath, stepping closer to place a hand on my shoulder. I turned to look up at her.

"Ion, there's something so different about you." Her voice came out soft and a little sad. "Don't ever lose that—don't ever be like the rest of us."

Her voice turned watery as she spoke the last words. She went silent for a moment before clearing her throat a little, sweeping up her composure. "I'll be downstairs if you need something, okay?"

I nodded, giving her a weak smile as she turned, swiping her index fingers beneath her eyes.

I waited there, still hugging my backpack to my chest, until I heard her footsteps on the stairs. Then I let go of the backpack and slid out of the chair to the floor, blowing out a long sigh. I lay there for a moment, staring up, watching my backpack drift up to bump against the ceiling tiles like a helium balloon.

ELEVEN

THE GROUND BLURRED PAST under my feet, muddy and uneven, sucking at my sneakers, making it harder and harder to take the next step. My heart thrashed in my chest, everything out of focus around me. A voice made me turn and look over my shoulder, snagging me in my tracks.

There was nothing there. Just shadows of the tall trees around me, curving and blinking like flickering images on an old TV screen.

"You're so different…" a soft familiar voice echoed. "Don't lose that… never lose that… never lose that…"

I pressed my head between my hands, feeling like it would explode at any second as those words rewound and replayed like a broken record.

"You can't run forever, Ion…" Her voice softened to a whisper in my ear. I could feel its warmth against my skin. "You can't run from something that's *inside you…*"

I whipped around to face the direction the voice seemed to be emanating from.

"Stop!" My voice roared out of my throat. "St-stop saying that! Just leave me the hell alone! J-j-just leave!"

I felt hands around my throat. I tried to jerk away, but I couldn't. My hands flew up to my neck to wrench theirs away, but my fingers closed around thin air. I gasped for breath, but my lungs felt like they were collapsing on themselves.

"You cannot run from who you are…" the voice whispered, morphing, distorting. "No matter how hard you try, you cannot stop *feeling*…"

I gagged and choked, gasping for breath, trying desperately to free myself from the stranglehold around my throat. It seemed no matter what I did, though, I couldn't free myself from my attacker's deadly grasp. I felt myself slipping away into darkness.

I jolted awake, tangled in the sheets, coughing and choking and sheathed in sweat. I sat upright, clutching my forehead. I felt sick to my stomach.

I took a deep breath—then choked again. I reached over and turned on the lamp by my bed, my heartbeat quickening as the room illuminated. Wisps of smoke hung in the air.

Throwing back the sheets, I leapt out of bed, bursting through the door and out into the hallway. A bright, flickering orange glow illuminated the walls of the stairwell.

"Fire!" I shouted, my eyes burning from the smoke. "There's a fire!"

I felt my way down the staircase, covering my mouth with the inside of my elbow. I felt my way through the kitchen to the hallway where Rachel's bedroom was. I could hear Gabe on the other side of the door, barking like mad. I kicked the door open and grabbed him before he had a chance to bolt.

"Rachel—up, now!" I shouted.

I could see her shadow in the glow from her pink night-light. "Wh-what's happening—"

"There's a fire! Come on!" With my free arm, I scooped her up and carried her to the back door, where I set her down and handed her the dog. "Stay outside!"

I ran back through the smoky house.

"Ion? Ion where are you?" Ava was pounding down the stairs, coughing and choking, her voice frantic.

"I'm in the—" I began, but didn't finish, gagging into my elbow as I ran into the living room. Through the thick haze of smoke, I could see that the TV stand was on fire, and the flames were starting to feed their way to the carpet. In their eerie glow, my eyes caught on a figure sprawled out on the couch.

"Mr. Reeves!" I shouted, diving across the room to shake him roughly. "Mr. Reeves, come on, wake up! There's a fire!"

When he didn't budge, I turned around and grabbed the half-filled glass of liquid on the coffee table, throwing it into his face. He started awake, gagging and spluttering.

"There's a fire!" I shouted, yanking him to his feet.

"Ion, look out!" Ava shouted, coughing and holding a fire extinguisher. Mr. Reeves stumbled through the kitchen and out the back door.

I stepped aside and Ava activated the extinguisher, letting loose a long stream of foam, sweeping it back and forth. I could hear Michael in the other room, yelling on the phone.

"Ion, get outside!" Ava shouted, spraying down the flames.

I shook my head, stepping up beside her. "Not until you do!"

In thirty seconds, the flames were cut down to hissing, simmering embers. She sprayed for a few more seconds before she eased off the trigger, shoving me back. "Alright, outside—let's go!"

The air was cold but sweet after I'd inhaled so much smoke. My lungs felt like they were on fire as I doubled over, coughing and gagging. Ava scooped Rachel up in her arms. I walked into the yard a little ways before dropping down on the ground, focusing on breathing. Out of the corner of my eye, I could see a neighbor talking to Mr. Reeves.

Moments later I heard sirens.

———

It was dawn by the time the fire department left. I was so tired that I'd crawled into the back of Ava's truck and passed out across the seats. Rachel was curled up on the bench seat in the front. I didn't wake up until I heard the loud, grumbling diesel engine roar to life. I rolled over, nestling my face in the worn, nicotine-scented fabric. The smell of smoke instantly made me feel sick to my stomach.

I rolled over onto my back, barely conscious. My muscles felt stiff and sore, and my brain felt like oatmeal in my clouded head. Sucking in a deep breath, I rubbed my bleary eyes, peeling them open begrudgingly one at a time. The stained ceiling of the truck slowly came into clear focus. I could hear the gruff voice of one of the firefighters talking to Ava.

I stared up at the ceiling of the truck, feeling numb. The circulation in my too-long legs had long since gone in the small space, leaving me with a pins-and-needles sensation; a seatbelt buckle was digging into my side, to top it all off.

So this was how they'd found me... whoever had discovered me lying there in the backseat of the wrecked car...

I squeezed my eyes shut and pulled myself up to sit, leaning back against the window.

Why had I been there? It was a question that had followed and taunted me like a demon ever since I'd been old enough to understand what the story meant, and how strange it made me. *Why hadn't they ever found the driver? Cars don't just wreck themselves...*

I'd never liked sitting in the backseat because of it. It made me think about it every time. I almost wished no one had ever told me how I was found.

Rachel moaned and grumbled in the front seat as the fire truck pulled away from the sidewalk and roared down the street. A moment later, her little blond head bobbed above the seats in front of me. She squinted at me with tired blue eyes.

"You awake?" she whispered groggily.

"What does it look like?"

She smirked a little. "What an exciting night."

I quirked an eyebrow. "You're a little bit psycho, you know that, Rach?"

She dove back below the seats, that same grin still on her face. "I can tell all the kids at school."

The priorities of little kids.

"Momma said you were the one who woke everyone up—you even saved Daddy."

My gaze ventured back up to the ceiling as I tipped my head back against the cold window. "Not really. The fire wasn't big or anything. Your mom would have woken him up as soon as she got downstairs."

"But you were the first one to wake up," she insisted.

"Alright, I'll give you that."

"Did you wake up because of the magic?"

I stifled a yawn. "What?"

"The magic," she repeated, matter-of-fact. "Is that why you woke up first?"

I had to think about what the hell she was saying for a moment before I finally remembered: Rachel thought I was magical.

"Is it because you were touched by the sun?" she pressed. "Does it make you more in tune with fire?"

I dragged a hand over my face, tugging at my lower eyelids. "Yup. That's it."

"I knew it!"

"Shhh. Remember what I said?"

Her hand cropped up above the seats again, her pinky sticking out as a reminder of our pact. "I haven't told anyone!"

"Good." I sighed, cranking my neck to look out the window. "Keep it that way. You wouldn't want the magic to wear off Gabe's leg."

She lifted the dog into her lap and started playing with his ears, making no response.

Ava walked over to the truck, zipping up her fleece. She tapped on my window, and I shimmied away from the door so she could open it.

"We can go back inside now," she announced, rubbing her hands together to keep warm. "They aired it out."

"Will the fire start again?" Rachel inquired, sounding a little too eager as she craned her neck to look at her mother.

Ava shook her head. "No, it won't start again. Everything's been taken care of." She blew out a sigh and turned to squint at the house. "Though there's quite a few repairs to be done..."

"I would think your insurance would cover the damage," I mused aloud. "Right?"

Ava nodded absently. "Should."

I slid out of the backseat and took a gulp of fresh air, slamming the door shut behind me. I looked at Ava.

"They figure out what caused the fire?" I asked.

Ava studied the front of the house for a long moment, then heaved a tired sigh. "According to one of the firefighters, Michael's gaming console overheated," she replied, rubbing her forehead, her eyes still fixed on the house. "That's what they think caused the fire."

I stared at her, stunned—a lead weight instantly dropping into my stomach. Ava bobbed her head in a slow nod when she noticed my surprise.

"It's horrifying, how something so unnoticeable and insignificant has the capacity to cause such harm," she mused, her voice edged with fatigue. "And Michael swears he hadn't left anything running when he'd gone to bed…"

My tongue was stuck to the roof of my mouth. I couldn't speak.

"Thank God you woke up when you did, Ion," she finally concluded, reaching over to put a hand on my shoulder. "Who knows what could have happened."

My mind was racing, along with my heart. I tried to respond, but it was like someone had shut off the flow of words to my brain.

Rachel tapped on the passenger window, smooshing her face against it. Ava walked over to pop it open, taking Gabe from her arms so she could easily slide to the ground. Rachel shot me a glance and tapped the side of her nose twice.

Ava followed Rachel's gaze to me and quirked an eyebrow. "What's that all about?" she asked as Rachel skipped toward the house.

I swallowed the lump that was forming in my throat, reaching up to wipe away the droplets of sweat that had sprung up across my forehead.

"N-nothing." My voice came out a little hoarse. "You know how Rachel likes to goof around."

Ava grunted a laugh. "She seems almost excited about the fire, the crazy child." She tipped her head in the direction of the house. "C'mon, let's head inside."

I shook my head, still rooted to the place I'd been standing. "I can't."

Ava's expression turned puzzled. I cleared my throat.

"I mean, I just have a headache," I explained. "From the smoke. I think I'll just take a little walk if that's okay with you?"

She seemed to consider it for a moment before nodding. "Alright. Want me to grab you a sweatshirt?"

I shook my head. "I'm fine."

"You sure?"

I nodded, numb.

Finally, Ava let me go with one last reminder not to go too far.

I barely comprehended the ground passing beneath my feet, or where I was going. My head really was pounding from the smoke, and my stomach churned. Despite the cool, early morning air, I was sweating bullets.

Only one thing kept racing through my mind, sending pain rattling through my skull: those thoughts I'd had the afternoon before of destroying Michael's gaming console. I'd imagined it exploding—melting. Bursting into flames. I'd relished those mental images, painting them in my mind like works of art as he sat there sneering at me.

I'd wished I could actually do those things. I'd wished it with all my heart, because I didn't know how else to fight back. I didn't know what else to do.

Exactly what I'd imagined had happened. There was no way in hell that was a coincidence. *No way.*

Walking down Main Street, I tried to ignore the blurs of my own reflection as I walked past closed shop windows, Ava's words ricocheting around in my brain like bullets:

"It's horrifying, how something so unnoticeable and insignificant has the capacity to cause such harm..."

Horrifying.

Insignificant.

Harmful.

The words pounded with the headache, with my every heavy footstep. I picked up my pace.

Horrifying.

Insignificant.

Harmful.

I broke into a run, tearing down the sidewalk, blurs of my reflection still seeming to taunt me—seeming to scream at the top of their lungs:

Harmful,

Harmful,

Harmful.

My stomach lurching, I cut a sharp left into a quiet alley, where I leaned against the wall and threw up what little I had inside me onto the ground. My whole body was shaking, and sweat was dripping off my face as I slid to my knees, dragging my trembling fingertips across the brick.

Tears welled in my eyes as I knelt there for a moment, gasping for breath. My hands felt like they were burning.

What if I hadn't woken up? What if the house had burned— what if I'd killed them all?

I pressed the heels of my hands to my temples, breathing hard, trying to slow my mind down, but it was impossible. The subtle sounds of traffic and voices had muffled to nothing. All I could hear was my own ragged breathing and what Ava had said.

Then a voice cut through the chaos.

"Ion?"

I didn't respond. I couldn't. I just stared down at the ground, finally feeling nothing at all.

Until two hands closed around my arms and hoisted me up to my feet.

TWELVE

"HERE'S THE TEA with milk and sugar, and here's the large black coffee." The waitress slid our respective drinks in front of us. "Can I get you guys anything else?"

We were sitting in a booth toward the back of the sleepy diner on the corner of Fifth and Main. The old guy sat across from me, wearing a sweatshirt and a beat-up ball cap. He shook his head and smiled. "That's it for now," he replied, his voice as calm and casual as ever. "Thanks."

She bobbed her head in a nod and walked off, leaving me to stare down at the mug of steaming black liquid in front of me. For a moment I just sat there with my eyes closed and inhaled the steam as it wafted up into my face. The jukebox at the far end of the diner was playing "I Feel Free," and I was feeling anything but.

"Feeling any better?" the old man asked.

I shrugged one shoulder. "Incrementally…" I opened my eyes and squinted at him. He took a long draught from the mug in front of him. "What were you doing in that alley anyway?" I asked.

He drank in silence for a moment before setting the mug down and wiping his mouth with the back of his hand.

"Came into town to get groceries," he said, tipping back his head to pass me a certain look. "What about you?"

"Throwing up," I answered flatly. "What did it look like?"

The old guy didn't say anything in response. I picked up the spoon beside my cup to dip it into the coffee and swirl it around aimlessly.

"I had to get away from the house," I said finally, my voice raw and honest. "I… couldn't stand to look at it."

"Oh?" asked the old man. "And why's that?"

My eyes followed the swirling motions of the dark liquid. "I'm too ashamed to talk about it…" I paused, shaking my head. "No, not even ashamed… More like terrified."

The old man didn't say anything. I could tell he was waiting for me to go on.

"You know, that day you first saw me on the beach…" I paused and took a deep breath. "I was thinking about walking straight into that lake… just walking until the water was up over my head, until I was as deep under as I feel right now."

My gaze flicked up to find the old man nodding steadily.

"I know," he said. "That's why I stopped you."

I looked at him for a moment, puzzled. "How could you have known something like that?"

"Because I could see the despair in you, oozing out like infection from a wound." He leaned forward a little, pushing up his sleeves and resting his bony elbows on the table. "This…" He tapped his temple with his index finger. "This is where the infection starts— in your thoughts… in your mind. Yet this same place can also be the source of everything good and worthwhile."

"There's nothing good or worthwhile in me," I replied bitterly. "The last few days have shown me that. I… I told you I don't want to talk about it—that I can't, but…"

"But what?"

"But I have bad thoughts—bad feelings," I blurted, my voice cracking a little. "I feel out of control, like—like I can't stop thinking! I can't stop feeling the way I do…" I dragged a hand down my face. "Like you said, the infection leaks out… and it's contagious. It screws with reality and turns it into a nightmare—like my thoughts aren't just thoughts, like they—"

"Have lives of their own?"

My gaze flashed to the old man's. "Exactly."

He nodded, sipped his tea. "Thoughts are never just thoughts, Ion. Look around you… Everything that you can see, everything that you can touch, everything that you can hear… everything—it was all once just a silent thought. Just an unspoken feeling."

I was confused, but I was listening. I watched his blue eyes flicker back and forth as he looked around at everything, as though he were admiring our humble environment.

"Thoughts are like… well, they're like any living, breathing thing—plants, for instance," he went on. "If you water it, give it plenty of sunlight, feed it, and spend time with it every day, it will grow into a strong, healthy plant. If you neglect it, fail to water it, and hide it away in the shadows, it will wither and fade away to dust."

"So what does that mean, exactly?" I asked.

"It means that we get to choose which thoughts to water," he answered. "Which thoughts to put out in the sun. We're the gardeners of our own minds."

"Well, in that case my garden's overgrown with thorn bushes," I said, finally picking up my mug to take a few steady sips. "I think it's turning me into a monster of some kind."

"The wind carries seeds from everywhere, spreading them over the earth in all directions," he replied. "We cannot control the wind; she breathes and blows wherever she wants to. We can't control which seeds scatter across our soil. But we can control what we do with them..."

"Which ones grow...?" I finished for him, shooting him a questioning look.

He nodded. "We all have bad thoughts and feelings sometimes. It's *what you do with them* that matters."

"What about when your thoughts hurt other people?" I lowered my gaze to my mug, to my hands around it. "What about when your feelings seem to destroy everything you come in contact with?" My fingers wound a little more tightly around the mug. "How do you stop feeling?"

"You don't," he said bluntly. "That would be asking something impossible of yourself. You will always think and feel—you just have to watch which thoughts you are allowing to grow. Grow only the ones that will make you stronger."

I heaved a tired sigh and took another sip from the mug. "Easier said than done."

"Yes, that's true," the old man agreed. "But like anything, it takes practice."

I shot him a glance. "I can't help but wonder sometimes if I'll always feel this lost. I always have—ever since I was old enough to know that I came from nowhere." I massaged my forehead with the heel of my hand. "Sometimes I wonder if I'll ever... figure myself out."

Tipping back the mug, I drained the rest of the coffee. The old man watched me, waiting until I had refocused on him before finally answering.

"One day you *will* figure yourself out, Ion," he said, his expression serious as he looked me square in the eyes. "So live for that… Don't you dare give up on yourself now."

The strange urgency of his voice took me a little aback. I considered what he was saying for a moment, my mind drifting back to waking up choking on smoke, running downstairs to find the living room splashed in flames.

I squeezed my eyes shut, pushing the imagery to the back of my mind. Taking a deep breath, I got up from the booth. I could feel the old man still studying me from where he sat, waiting for a response to what he'd just said.

Instead, I just gave him a nod and said, "Thanks for the coffee."

It wasn't until I got back to the Reeveses' house that I realized I'd once again forgotten to ask the old guy what his name was.

The scent of smoke still lingered in the air. Mr. Reeves was helping Ava clean up from the fire. Ava pointed a finger at me when I stepped through the front door.

"Thought I told you not to go far," she reprimanded me through her dust mask.

I apologized and asked if there was anything I could do to help, but Mr. Reeves made it abundantly clear that the last thing he wanted to endure, on top of everything else, was my presence. So I trudged upstairs.

The door to Michael's room was open, and I could see him inside, lying on his bed, staring up at the ceiling. I looked the other way just as fast, popping open the door to my room. But it wasn't fast enough.

"Hey, freakface."

I froze halfway over the threshold. My fingers tightened around the knob.

"I know you're standing right there." His voice continued to waft out of his room, cold and steely. "I know you can hear me."

I should have continued into the room—slammed the door shut behind me. But that strange, hot feeling filling my gut nailed me to the floor.

"First the dog... now this," he went on in the same tone. "What's it going to be next? One of us dying in our beds?"

The muscles in my neck tightened. I heard the rustling of sheets, and a moment later Michael appeared in the doorway. He watched me carefully.

"Dad and Ava might have bought whatever cover story you spat at them, but I sure as hell don't." He crossed his arms and leaned against the side of the door. "I'm the one you punched in the face, Ion—with the force of a goddamn freight train. I'm the one who punched the shit out of your face—only to find you looking normal a couple of hours later..."

Still I said nothing. My fingers felt hot as they curled around the cool brass knob.

"And yeah, Rachel's a nutcase, but she's not one to lie," he continued. "I saw Gabe's leg myself. I know you did something to it—"

"I did *nothing*."

"—and now this," he cut back in, his tone a little fiercer. "A strange fire starts in the middle of the night… and guess who's the first one—the *only* one—up?"

My throat tightened as I took a step back into the hallway.

"I woke up because of the smoke," I replied, my voice hard and trembling. "I went downstairs and saw the fire—that's exactly what happened."

Michael dropped his head in a slow, mocking nod. "I'll believe that when hell freezes over."

Everything inside me was beginning to boil. My face was hot, and that same heat was filling my hands like boiling liquid. I tried to stop myself—to mute the feelings and the thoughts in my head. I tried to uproot them, but they only grew deeper with the fire inside me.

Lunging forward, I grabbed Michael by the collar of his shirt and shoved him back against the wall.

"I didn't start the fire." My words rushed out in a violent whisper, my face mere inches from his. "I didn't heal the dog. I didn't do *anything*—do you understand? I didn't mean to hurt you—I never meant to hurt *anyone*."

He studied my face for a moment, looking completely unsurprised. After a moment, a smile twitched at his lips.

"Maybe you don't mean to." He lowered his voice. "But look at yourself…" He reached up and wrenched one of my hands off his collar. "Something inside you craves it…"

The hot feeling inside me slowly ebbed away. I felt as if I'd suddenly dropped back into my senses. I tore my focus from his eyes for a moment, realizing what I was doing: choking him.

Startled, I jerked backward, trying to put some distance between us, but he kept hold of my arm, twisting it and digging his nails in.

"I know there's something wrong with you, Ion," he hissed into my ear. "And I promise you… I will find a way to prove it."

I winced as he tweaked my arm once more, violently, before releasing me with a jerk. I staggered backward into my room, slamming the door shut behind me, locking it.

I thudded back against it and slid to the floor, then sat there for what felt like forever, staring at the empty space filling the distance between me and the other side of the room—the desk where my notebook was lying with a pencil next to it.

"Thoughts are never just thoughts…"

The old man's words rang through my head—the long, strange conversation we'd had over coffee. It felt like it was a dream. Like it hadn't really happened.

Thoughts grow. Thoughts make everything. And I chose which ones grew in my mind. That was what he'd told me—that I could control it.

But if that was true, then why couldn't I stop? Why couldn't I get back in control?

All I wanted was to fight this thing—to beat it before I lost my mind completely.

My thoughts froze there as something seemed to click at last. *Fighting it…*

What if that was where I was going wrong? What if rejecting it—fighting it—was what was making me spin out of control? The fighting, the fear… That was what grabbed me by the throat each time and held me down in a strangle grip. I'd tried as hard as I could to pull my feelings out by the roots; now I was starting to wonder if they were meant to grow.

Maybe if I stop fighting it… it would stop fighting me.

I drew a deeper breath, rolling my shoulders back. My gaze fixed on the desk across the room—on the pencil beside the notebook.

For a moment I didn't do anything. I just sat there, staring across the room at the pencil, thinking, until finally my mind fixated on one word:

Levitate.

I spun the word in my brain like thread, weaving a clear mental image: the same one that had haunted me since that first day everything had crashed and shattered.

That pencil peeling up off the floor to hover in midair, rising to meet my fingertips.

Levitate,

Levitate,

Levitate…

I visualized it in my mind, tipping my head back against the door and squeezing my eyes shut. The heat in my hands reignited, warmth flowing down my arms and creeping into my fingertips. I lifted one of my hands and held it out in front of me, spreading my fingers wide, breathing deep the dizzy feeling that was washing over me like a crashing waterfall.

My hand trembled and shook. A moment later, something brushed up against my palm. My fingers snapped closed around it, and I bolted upright again, my eyelids flying open. My heart dammed up the back of my throat.

The pencil was in my hand.

THIRTEEN

I started doing this—writing down the things I think and feel—because I didn't know what else to do with the mess inside me. This is an outlet—something to help me fight the way I feel; to keep it contained. But it almost feels like the more I try to do that, the worse it gets—the harder it fights back. And the more I feel like I'm on the losing side.

The pencil levitated again, but this time I did it on purpose. I don't know what to do. I'm so scared... I'm scared of myself. I never thought I would say that, but I am.

I wish I'd just told the old man everything—he's the only one who seems to get me, somehow. There's something about him: I feel like I can actually... talk to him. But I'd just been so afraid that he would just push me away too if he knew the truth about me, if he knew that I'd started the fire.

I started the fire. I know I did, so does Michael. I could have killed everyone—what if I had?

That's not even what bothers me the most. What terrifies me more than anything is this feeling inside me that this is just the beginning. Ever since the pencil levitated for the first time, everything has only gotten more tripped out. I feel like I'm constantly high—I wish I were. At least that would explain it all.

I feel like someone else is living in my body. And I don't know what's going to happen next.

I don't know.

———————

I lay awake for hours, breathing in the subtle smell of ash still lingering in the air.

Fire,

Fire,

Fire.

My fault.

I listened to a car passing outside, the mournful howl of a train in the distance, calling my name like a siren at sea, beckoning me into the darkness, seeming to whisper temptations: *vanish.*

I tucked my hands behind my head, breathing steadily, staring up at the ceiling in the dark. The train blew its whistle again, this time slipping down the throat of the night and fading to silence. I wished I were on that train, regardless of where it was going. It would be anywhere but here.

I pressed my eyes closed, letting go of the breath I hadn't realized I'd been holding. Muffled voices from downstairs began to mix with the moonlight. I couldn't make the words out, not from there. I listened for a moment before I slid out from between the sheets. The floor was cool under my bare feet as I moved across the room and down the stairs in silence.

I stopped at the second-to-last step, leaning back against the wall. I heard the refrigerator door open.

"Mike, please." Ava's voice was quiet. "Come sit down. Talk to me."

The *psshht* of a can cracking open. Chair legs dragging across the linoleum.

"I already said everything I have to say," he mumbled. He sounded tired.

"Well, *I* haven't."

Mr. Reeves muttered something inaudible under his breath, taking a swig of his beer.

"You were standing right there, Mike. You heard what the firefighter said," Ava went on, her fighting tone on. "He told us that Michael's gaming console overheated and caught fire."

"All by itself like that?" He grunted skeptically. "Isn't that a little strange?"

"Michael may have left it running."

"He says he didn't."

"You and I both know he can be careless."

"You and I both know that there's something strange about that boy," Reeves countered coldly.

"Ion? Mike, what the hell? You're blaming an innocent kid who has been through a lot more than you realize." The words rushed out of Ava like an angry river. "I can't believe you would let their little rivalry cloud your judgment—Michael's just jealous. He'll get over it."

"Michael said Ion punched him in the face at school—"

"Which wasn't true, obviously—Michael also said he punched Ion back, but Ion looked just fine when he came home that day. You and I were both standing right there. You saw the same thing I did."

There was a pause. Mr. Reeves slammed his can down on the table a moment later, making me jump a little.

"My son doesn't lie."

Ava didn't say anything at first. I leaned a little closer.

"He was probably embarrassed that someone at school got the better of him—you know how much he likes to look tough and capable. He was just trying to save face in front of his dad."

"No—no, he would never say that that scrawny little bastard of a kid punched him in the face if it didn't actually happen," Mr. Reeves protested. "There's no goddamn way he lied about that."

"I don't think Ion did anything. I know him, Mike."

"Ava, he's been here three months—you don't know anything about this kid!"

"Well, I've certainly spent more time trying to get to know him than you have!"

Mr. Reeves grunted. "He's just a foster kid, Ava—why would I try to get to know him? He could be gone in a week. And honestly? That would be alright with me. At least I wouldn't have to worry about him knifing one of us in our sleep."

I pulled back into the shadows a little, swallowing back the impact the words had, in spite of my efforts to deflect them.

Ava cursed, slamming something. "How the hell can you say that? How can you be so cruel?"

"I'm not cruel; I'm realistic," he said. "Who was the first one up when the fire started?"

No reply.

"Ion," Mike answered for her. "Who's the one who fought with Michael at school? Ion. Who's the one who had Rachel in a frenzy over that stupid dog? Ion—"

"Ion said he didn't do anything to the dog."

"Yet he spent the night in Rachel's room."

"He was helping, Mike. I saw—I went in to check on Rachel and I talked to him."

"What about after you left? How do you know *what* he was doing to our daughter when you weren't looking?"

The sharp sound of a slap suddenly cut through the quiet.

"How can you say things like that?" she roared, sobbing. "How can you even think it? When he's done nothing to deserve it!"

A long pause. A chair pushing back.

"If you don't call the agency and have them send someone down here, I will." His tone was hard and unmoving. "I want that boy dealt with."

"There's nothing to deal with! Don't you see that?" She was crying now; I could tell. "How can you not see that?"

I held my breath, waiting to see how he would respond. He walked across the room and threw his empty can away; I heard the trash can lid close.

"What did he tell you when you asked him about Rachel and her dog?" His tone hardened with the question.

"He said that he didn't do anything to the dog," Ava replied.

Another pause, then Reeves's voice. "So what was he really doing in her room that night, then?"

There was a long, long silence this time. And that was where the conversation ended.

Ava didn't answer.

FOURTEEN

WHEN THE SCHOOL BUS pulled up in front of the Reeveses' house the next afternoon, Michael shoved me down the steps and I face-planted in the driveway.

"Oops!" he said as he jumped over me, continuing toward the house.

The bus driver asked if I was alright. I said I was fine, I was fine.

I wasn't. But it had nothing to do with my muddy, bruised knees.

I quickly got back up, a fresh dose of hot blood rushing to my face. There was an extra car in the driveway. A little white Prius.

A weight sank into my gut as I stood there, clutching the strap of my backpack while the bus rolled away.

I didn't want to go in. I wanted to run.

But if I ran now, I would look guilty as shit. Ava would believe her husband, and this would be over. She'd been the first person in a long time to treat me like I was normal. I didn't want to lose that.

I squeezed my eyes shut, sucked in a deep breath, and pushed myself forward across the driveway and up the steps. I slid my backpack off in the mudroom along with my shoes. I could hear voices in the living room; Mr. Reeves and someone else. As soon as I stepped into the room, a woman stood up. She was tall, with a round face and wavy red hair. She was wearing a crisp white button-down shirt, slacks, and those glossy clogs moms wear. She smiled when she saw me.

"You must be Ion," she said.

I looked at her for a moment, my stomach in knots. "Who are you?"

"I'm Brigid." She took a few steps to stick out her hand for me to shake. "I'm here from child services. It's nice to meet you."

I dipped my head in a slow nod, shooting Mr. Reeves a glance. He was sitting on the couch with his arms crossed over his chest. His eyes hardened when they met mine.

"I thought we could chat a little if that's okay with you," Brigid went on, her lilting tone masking something serious she didn't want me to notice. "Want to head into the kitchen?"

I shook my head, my eyes still locked with Mr. Reeves's. "My room," I answered. "If that's okay with you."

Brigid followed my gaze, then looked back at me. She nodded and gestured for me to lead the way.

My feet felt heavier than usual as I climbed the stairs, the quiet clicking of the nice social worker's clogs following me up to my room, where I shut the door. I immediately walked over to my desk and shoved my notebook and pencil into a drawer. I pulled the desk chair out and asked her if she'd like to sit.

She looked a little taken aback, but after a second, she sat down. "Thank you."

I perched on the edge of my bed, leaning forward to rest my elbows on my knees, and looked at her.

"How are things going?" she asked.

"Fine," I said.

"Mr. Reeves says you and Michael have been fighting a lot."

"No more than we usually do."

"He says you hit Michael… Is that true?"

I shook my head. "No, ma'am."

She looked at me for a long moment, seeming to study my eyes.

"Has Michael ever hit you?" she asked finally.

I shook my head. "I told you, everything is fine. Michael is whatever… We don't hang out."

Brigid quirked one eyebrow. "Yet you're happy here?"

I was about to answer, but the words swelled and faded in my throat. I closed my eyes for a moment and took a deep breath.

My hands were shaking a little, but this time it wasn't from that strange, warm rush of energy I'd begun to grow used to. This time it was just because I was coming apart inside.

The truth was, I couldn't remember ever being happy. I wasn't even sure I knew what it felt like.

All the things that made most people happy—a family, a friend, someone or something to hold onto when you're crumbling; someone to talk to when it felt like no one in the world would listen, someone to tell "I love you"—I'd never experienced any of those things. I didn't know what it meant to be loved, or even liked, really. I didn't know what the warmth of a real hug felt like. I didn't know what it felt like to *have someone* to hug…

I didn't know what it felt like to *have someone*. Because, every day, I was reminded that these people around me were temporary, that I couldn't get used to them. It was only a matter of time until they figured out that, despite all my lies, something *was* wrong with me. Mr. Reeves was right: I *was* dangerous.

No one wanted a dangerous boy in their house.

"Ion?"

I sucked in a deep breath, blinking and refocusing on the young woman who was still waiting for an answer. "Yeah," I whispered, forcing a nod. "I'm happy here."

She gave me a look I couldn't decipher and sat back in her chair. "Rachel said you spent the night sleeping on the floor in her room when her dog was sick."

"She was exhausted, but she didn't want to leave his side. So I stayed up with him."

Brigid looked away for a moment, as though she were hesitating. "And did you touch Rachel?"

Anger swelled inside me. My fingertips twitched.

When I closed my eyes, I immediately saw Mr. Reeves's face; I could hear echoes of his voice. His hateful whispers—the lies he'd told Ava. I felt every bit as sick as I had when I'd stood there in the shadow of the stairwell, listening. Taking the bullets.

I took a narrow breath, looking her right in the eyes for a long moment before shaking my head. "No, ma'am," I said. "I did not."

"Okay," Brigid replied quietly, her voice unreadable. "Okay, I just needed to check up on that."

"Any other questions?"

"There was a fire here recently—I saw the damage in the living room," she answered. "Mr. Reeves said you were the first one to wake up. Is that true?"

"I woke up because of the smoke, yeah."

"What did you do after you woke up?"

"I yelled 'fire' in the hall and ran downstairs. I went to Rachel's room first and helped her outside, and then I ran into the living room, where I saw the TV stand was on fire. I woke Mr. Reeves up—he was passed out on the couch."

"And then?"

"Then Ava and Michael came downstairs. Michael called the fire department and Ava grabbed the fire extinguisher," I said, wrapping up the explanation. "They think it's because the gaming console overheated."

"Had you been playing video games?"

"No. Michael had."

Brigid's expression was still unreadable. "And you weren't downstairs before the fire? Mr. Reeves thinks you might have been."

"I was not."

The social worker folded her hands on her knees, studying me for a long moment before drawing a breath. "How are the Reeveses treating you?"

"Fine."

"What about Mr. Reeves—do you have a good relationship with him?"

I shrugged. "We don't spend time together, but we're fine. There's nothing wrong."

She seemed to consider it for a moment before tipping her head toward the door. "Let's head downstairs."

She waited around for Ava to get home from work and had a long talk with her at the kitchen table. I listened on the bottom of the steps.

"Ion seems fine," she said. "I think you guys don't have much to worry about—keep an eye on him and keep us updated if you think there's anything off about his behavior. His story matches

Rachel's: he was watching the dog while she slept, and he fell asleep himself."

"Even so, that doesn't take care of the issues pertaining to my son," Mr. Reeves replied before Ava could. "Ion punched him."

"We don't know that for sure," Ava cut in firmly. "I think Michael's trying to get our attention."

"It's possible—likely, even," Brigid said. "You'll find that the dynamic of your family, and even the attitudes of your children, may adjust a little; you have another child in the house now. It can often take time for the other children within the home to settle." Her tone was calm and matter-of-fact. "We've never had reports of any issues with Ion before."

"I thought this was the first time you'd met him," Mr. Reeves interrupted. "How the hell would you know?"

"We keep meticulous records on each child, Mr. Reeves," Brigid said firmly. "And according to the information we have from the other families Ion has been with, he's never overstepped his boundaries—if anything, he's a bit standoffish. He seems content living here. I think you have little reason to believe he would try to start a fire, or mistreat your other children—especially when your own children seem to have no complaints about him."

One of the kitchen chairs pushed back.

"I'll go upstairs and talk with Michael, if that's alright," she continued. "But from what I'm seeing, it seems like their rivalry isn't out of hand. Many biological siblings are that way."

Mr. Reeves started to object, but Ava cut in. "You'll find him in his room."

I quickly crept back up the stairs and slipped into my room, closing the door behind me. I slid to the floor and took a deep breath.

I couldn't hear the conversation that went down between Michael and the social worker, but twenty minutes later the Prius pulled out of the driveway and vanished down the street.

Things were okay for now.

Dinner was awkward. Ava didn't say much. Michael and his father talked about his day at school and sports. When dinner was over, everyone scattered, leaving Ava to clean up. I stayed behind to help.

Still, she didn't say anything for a long while. Finally, when she started washing dishes and handing them to me to dry, she turned to me. "Ion, it's important to me that you know that I trust you, and I had no doubts about the fact that you were helping Rachel with the dog that night," she said quietly. "It's just that—"

"Mr. Reeves doesn't trust me," I finished for her, circling the dish towel over the wet plate. "I know. It's okay."

She turned to look at me. "You're not upset about it?"

I set the plate down on the counter and took the next one from her. "I'm used to it…"

Ava didn't say anything in response right away; she just stood there with her soapy hands hovering over the sink, looking at me like I was still that tricky math problem.

I pulled in a shakier breath, meeting her gaze now. "I hope you know that I would never intentionally do anything to hurt anyone."

My heart pounded a little faster in my chest as I spoke the words. She didn't know that the keyword of what I'd just said was "intentionally."

The expression on Ava's face remained the same for a moment as she tried to read my eyes. Then she pressed her lips into a thin, sad smile and said, "I know that, Ion."

FIFTEEN

A FEW DAYS HAD passed since the social worker came. Nothing had happened since then: nothing had floated and I hadn't punched anyone. My hands had barely even shaken. I wrote in my journal every day, and I was beginning to think that maybe things would be different now that I'd begun to accept the fact that *I* was. Maybe embracing the strange things that happened would make them stop happening…

At least that was what I hoped.

Things between Michael and me were no better, but no worse either, and the following week, I stopped by the beach to talk to the old man. He sat on the log across from me and listened to what I had to say without judgment in his eyes. A fire crackled between us.

"I don't think Ava was the one who wanted the social worker to come; it was her husband. His son hates me, and he told his dad a bunch of bullshit about me that isn't even true," I explained, making scratch marks in the sand with a stick. "He tried to make it sound like I did something wrong. And I… I did do something wrong, but not to Rachel… I did something wrong to everyone, without meaning to. Has anything like that ever happened to you?" I asked, glancing at him over the flames. "Have you ever hurt someone without meaning to?"

"I think that's happened to everyone at some time or another," he answered. "Have you talked to the person you hurt? Have you told them you're sorry?"

I tipped my head to the side. "In a roundabout way. But it doesn't make up for what happened… and what could happen."

"What do you mean?"

"I mean that I'm afraid I'll do it again," I told the sand, digging at it with the stick. "I mean that I can't seem to stop… I tried. But it's like my thoughts choke out everything else in that mind-garden you talk about, until there's nothing left but thorns to shred me to pieces."

The old man became quiet and thoughtful.

"Please don't ask me to tell you anything more." I sighed, still studying the ground. "I can't… I haven't even told anyone this much before."

The old man gave a slow nod, then leaned forward on his knees to look at me through steady eyes. "Your mind is the strongest and most daunting opponent you will ever face, Ion." His voice was serious. "It will beat you down and hold you there if you let it. It will tell you that you are at its mercy because you *are* what you think about, but that's a lie."

I raised an eyebrow. "What do you mean?"

"Just what I've been telling you all along: you are not every thought that passes through your mind, or every feeling that rushes through your veins," he answered. "Just because there are leaves floating on the surface of the lake doesn't make them part of the lake. The lake is just a vehicle to carry them. Let go of the thoughts that hurt."

I looked back at the ground and shook my head slowly. I thought about how I'd focused on making the pencil levitate and float to my hand, and how I'd actually been able to do it. How that was the most in control I'd felt in a long time.

"Just because something makes you different, Ion," he began quietly, "does not mean that it makes you bad or dangerous."

"You have no idea what happened."

"I don't need to know what happened," he replied. "But you should consider that perhaps what you keep trying to reject about yourself is actually what you should be embracing; perhaps it's the thoughts that tell you that you are bad or dangerous that must be silenced in your mind."

I threw down the stick now, my gaze shooting up to meet his. "You don't know what it's like, okay? You have no idea! I could have killed them!" The words rushed off my lips before I could stop them. "You don't know what it's like to lie awake at night, being scared to death—repeating to yourself over and over and over again, *Don't think, don't think, don't think*—because you're afraid of what your next thought could do!"

The old man's expression didn't change; his eyes didn't flicker away from mine. I clasped my face in my hands, immediately regretting letting my guard down.

"Look, just—just forget I said anything." I was already getting to my feet, stepping around the fire. "Just forget about me—I should never have come to see you…" I stopped and turned to look at him. "I should never have talked to you in the first place—you talk about things you don't even understand, old man."

I turned to face forward, taking a step. He reached out and clasped a hand gently around my wrist.

My gaze shot to his. His blue eyes were as stormy as the churning navy sky over the lake.

"Ion, be careful." His voice was quiet but serious. I stood there, frozen for a moment.

I wrenched my hand away and began to run, my sneakers kicking up sand as I left him and the fire and that little driftwood hut behind. I ran all the way back to the Reeveses' house.

The house smelled of pasta and marinara sauce. Ava was in the kitchen and Mr. Reeves was passed out on the sofa.

"Hey, where have you been?" Ava glanced up from setting the table as I stepped in. "Michael said you missed the bus."

I nodded. "Intentionally. I wanted to go for a run on the beach."

"One of your teachers told me how much you like running," she said. "Maybe you should think about getting into track."

"Nah, I just do it to blow off steam." I slid off my backpack and dropped it on the floor. "Can I help?"

Ava shook her head. "Go take your stuff upstairs and wash your hands, please—and tell Michael it's time for dinner, alright?"

I picked up my backpack. "Alright."

I was already starting toward the stairs when she stopped me again. "Oh, and, Ion?"

I shot a glance over my shoulder at her. "Yeah?"

She set the last plate down and passed me a little smile. "Tell Rachel, too—she's playing in her room."

I felt frozen for a moment as I stood there on the threshold, staring at her. Then that feeling inside me began to slowly melt. For the first time in a very, very long time, I felt the corners of my mouth curve upwards just a little. My voice had a hard time getting past the lump in my throat.

"Okay," I said quietly. "Okay, I will."

I backtracked across the kitchen to the hallway where Rachel's room was. I paused to look back when I reached the doorway.

"Ava?"

She turned and looked at me over her shoulder. "Yes, Ion?"

For a moment the storm inside me began to disintegrate into a gentle rain that fell and settled over all the hard, cracked ground inside me. And for a moment, something felt right again. Something inside me began to feel like maybe—just maybe—things were starting to get better. Maybe things would actually be okay.

Maybe the last week had just been a bad dream. Maybe this was what waking up felt like.

I pulled in a shaky breath; my voice came out equally unsteady. "Thank you."

Ava didn't say anything, but she didn't need to. I could tell by the look in her eyes that I didn't have to be terrified of what was going to happen next, of another strange car pulling into the driveway, or another nice lady telling me to pack my things. I could tell that Ava trusted me again.

I felt ten times lighter as I turned and walked down the hallway, stopping at the door with the horse stickers. I lifted my hand to softly knock.

"Hey, Rachel, it's me—Ion."

There was a pause; then she chirped for me to come in. Gabe frolicked out as I eased the door open. I stepped into the room, which was bathed in dim pinkish light. Rachel was sitting cross-legged on her bed, surrounded by an army of stuffed animals.

"Ion, did you see Gabe?" she asked, pointing after the terrier. "Did you see how excited he was to see you?"

I nodded, swallowing back a nagging feeling in my gut, pushing on a smile for her sake. "Yeah," I said. "Yeah, he looks great. Hey, your mom wanted me to tell you it's time for dinner, okay?"

She didn't respond. She just tilted her head to one side and sat there gaping at me with big blue eyes.

"What?" I asked at last, stepping farther into the room. "What is it?"

She looked up at me, her eyebrows pressed together. "How come that lady came and asked me all those questions about you, Ion?" She sounded confused. "How come they thought you hurt me?"

I pulled in a deep breath and sat down on the edge of her bed. I folded my hands on my knees for a moment, staring down at them as I thought. Then I turned and looked her in the eyes.

"Sometimes people get afraid when something happens and they don't understand it," I told her softly. "Sometimes their gut reaction is to push it away before they even know the whole story. But sometimes…"

Her eyebrows rose a little when I trailed off; my throat felt tight.

"Sometimes what?" she asked, staring at me like whatever I was about to say would be a message straight from God.

My lips formed a weak smile as I swallowed back the lump in my throat. "Sometimes different doesn't necessarily mean bad," I finished quietly. "Just because we don't understand something doesn't mean it's wrong… It just means it's different."

Rachel's tiny pink lips curled into a grin. "Like how you can heal—"

"Shhh." I placed a finger to my lips but nodded. "Like that."

She pretended to zip her lips, though the grin didn't fade. I smiled a little.

"Maybe it took you to make me realize that, Rach," I said quietly. "You and Gabe… and…"

A heavy feeling drifted into my stomach when I thought of the old man; how I'd yelled at him on the beach. He'd been the one to tell me the things no one else would, and I'd treated him like crap.

I snapped out of it, shaking my head, and got to my feet. "Come on. Better get washed up."

Rachel sighed and begrudgingly peeled herself up off the bed. She trudged out into the hallway, heading for the bathroom. She seemed to forget about how grumpy she was about having to leave her room as soon as Gabe came tearing down the hallway to find her.

"I'll be right down," I told Ava as I passed through the kitchen again.

I took the stairs two at a time, my bare feet light against the hardwood; I felt like something inside me was levitating.

I stopped at Michael's bedroom door, rapping softly with my knuckles.

"Hey, time for dinner," I said into the crack between the door and the threshold.

No answer.

I knocked again. "Hey, Michael?"

Still nothing.

This time I grasped the knob and twisted it, pushing the door open on the dimly lit disaster area. It was vacant.

I frowned, spinning back around to cross the hallway to my room. I pushed the door open—and everything came crashing to a halt.

Michael looked up from where he was standing at my desk. All the cold hatred had gone from his eyes, replaced by what I could only describe as terror. My notebook lay open in his hands.

SIXTEEN

I'D ALWAYS WONDERED what it would feel like to be caught up inside a tornado; what it would be like to feel hurricane-force winds sweeping me off my feet—the sky sucking me up through a stormy, gray straw, tossing me around in billows of oblivion—then to surface again above the clouds. That moment of sun-drenched suspension. That moment before the sky let me down again, back into the black, swirling chaos, dropping me to my death.

But the moment just before, everything goes weightless. That's when reality melts away, leaving you raw inside, ushering in an ending worse than any real Armageddon, because no one feels it but you. It is your own isolated apocalypse, that feeling before you fall— that moment of sunlight and blurry clouds. Then it's swallowed by darkness.

That was how I felt standing there in the doorway, staring into my bedroom lit only by the desk lamp. The soft tungsten light illuminated Michael's features as he stood there with my composition notebook spread open in his hands; it reflected in his wide eyes, where a storm as dark as any twister brewed. I felt frozen to the floor where I stood, like my muscles had atrophied to nothing. My lungs had lost the ability to breathe, and my mouth the ability to say anything that would redeem me.

I was irredeemable, and I knew it as soon as Michael stepped forward, snapping the book shut, closing the distance between us until he was just a few feet away. He set his jaw.

"Move," he barked in a strained voice as he tucked the book firmly under his arm.

If I hadn't been so numb, maybe I would have tried to talk him out of telling Mr. And Mrs. Reeves about it. Maybe I would have knocked him to the ground and wrestled it out of his hands. But those same old feelings had already regained their stranglehold on me, the familiar feeling that I was just about to fall.

Eventually, I managed a choked breath, forming it into one pleading and nearly silent word: "Please."

The voice that came out of my throat didn't even sound like my own; it sounded like someone else's. One simple word I could barely bring myself to audibly speak, yet it held my life story inside it. I'd heard it repeated in my head every time the world began to crumble around me—every time I saw a look in someone's eyes that said this was all about to end, that I was about to be spit out like something that just couldn't be swallowed.

Please.

Every new school, every first day; every hard, cold look; every cutting word—every shove to the ground and black-eye tattoo they used to label me *misfit*. Every time.

Please.

Every change of address, every sit-down conversation with some nice lady I'd never met before, asking me if everything was okay. Every time I met a new face, opening their front door and asking if they could help me with my bag—

Please.

And it wasn't so much a question or a plea as much as it was a gasping voice garbled by the slap of another suffocating wave—ragged lungs, lost at sea, surrounded by sharks and sinking deeper, deeper, deeper...

Please. I'm drowning.

Please... Don't throw me away.

But Michael's gaze only grew steelier. He pointed to the floor a few feet to one side and roared, "Move!" so hard that spit flew out of his mouth.

Wordlessly, I stepped aside. He strode past me out into the hallway, and a moment later I heard the hammering of his footfalls as he descended the stairs.

"Dad! Dad, we need to talk now!" His voice ripped through the air like a gunshot, impacting right into my chest.

I felt rooted to the floor where I'd been standing. My hands began to tremble and shake, but this time the warmth wasn't there. This time they felt stone cold.

My eyes caught on my reflection in the mirror across the room; hollow eyes stared back at me. Eyes that didn't know what the hell they were looking at.

Please... I'm drowning.

All my motions felt mechanical as I turned and walked out into the hallway, putting one foot in front of the other until I was out of my bedroom and down the stairs. Everything still smelled like pasta and warm bread, but now the scent turned my stomach.

Michael was standing in the middle of the kitchen, holding the notebook open in the air. Mr. Reeves was red-eyed and seemingly frozen, a beer can half lifted to his lips. Ava was standing at the stove, and the smile had vanished from her face.

"Maybe now you'll believe me!" Michael flashed the composition notebook around aggressively. "Maybe now you'll see him for the freak he really is!"

Ava stepped forward and wrenched the notebook out of Michael's hands. "What on earth are you talking about?"

I felt sick as I stood there, watching the tornado ripping toward me. My eyes made contact with Rachel's. She was already sitting at the table, her cheeks full of food. She smiled when she saw me and patted the chair beside her. My throat tightened and I shook my head.

Ava sucked in a deep breath, blowing it out again as she flipped through the pages. I could tell by the look on her face that she thought this was just another load of Michael's typical bullshit. Then suddenly she stopped turning the pages. Her blue eyes flicked back and forth as she read. She took a step back to lean against the counter, clutching it with her hand and squeezing her eyes shut.

"What is it?" Mr. Reeves finally demanded, slamming his can of beer down on the counter, sending some sloshing out. "Give that to me."

Ava didn't move—didn't even open her eyes, which were still clamped painfully shut—and Mr. Reeves didn't wait for her to respond. He tore the notebook out of her hands and read the page over for himself. Michael crossed his arms over his chest.

I could feel the thud, thud, thud of my heartbeat in the back of my head. A throbbing like an aftershock from a bomb detonating.

Mr. Reeves looked up from the notebook and stared at me, his eyes brimming with fury. It was the first time anyone had even noticed me standing there on the threshold, white as a ghost, silent as a ghost.

"You are a monster." His voice came out shaky and low. "Everything you told me not to worry about, Ava… everything you dismissed as bullshit—it was all true. That boy…" He jabbed a finger in my direction; it trembled almost as much as mine did. "That boy is a freak!"

He shouted so loud, I staggered backwards a step, feeling like I'd just been stabbed.

"I warned you!" he went on, his voice escalating as he took a step toward Ava. "I told you it would end this way—that we never should have taken him on. This is your fault!"

Ava recoiled from his shouting, clasping a hand over her eyes, her lips twisting into a miserable frown as she started to weep.

"Do you realize that?" Mr. Reeves went on screaming, leaning over Ava. "You brought him here—this is your fault, goddamn you!"

Rachel started crying, her tiny face turning bright red. "Daddy, stop! Stop it, please!"

Her screams ripped through my head like a migraine, but Mr. Reeves was deaf to them. Everything became a blur after that. My breath froze in my throat as Mr. Reeves surged forward, grabbing Ava by the shoulders, shaking her so hard her hair spilled out of its bun. Michael just stood there, but Rachel started screaming, clutching her face, her blue eyes wide and horrified.

I was in the tornado, spiraling downward into the darkness. This was what the darkness looked like… and I was the cause.

You are a monster.

I surged forward, my hands on fire, shaking so hard I felt like I was having a seizure. In a second, I was across the kitchen, latching onto Mr. Reeves, throwing myself between him and Ava. I drove the heels of my hands into his chest and shoved—hard.

Mr. Reeves went flying backwards, slamming into the wall at the opposite side of the room.

Boom-boom, boom-boom, boom-boom went my heart, like explosions in my chest.

I gasped for air, turning to look at Ava, who was still frozen, still horrified, black tears streaking down her face. Her eyes met mine, that same look still in them: like I was a problem—one she had finally solved.

You are a monster.

I turned slowly and looked at Rachel. Tears rolled down her cheeks. She stumbled backward and shielded her face as soon as our eyes met, terrified—

Terrified of *me*.

Mr. Reeves coughed and staggered to his feet. No one else moved in the silent, pulsating room. Michael stood by the door, the blood draining from his face.

The room froze, all the noise seeming to fade away.

Turning on my heel, I tore through the house, nearly tripping over the dog. The last thing I heard was Mr. Reeves yelling for someone to call the police. After that, I couldn't hear anything except the sounds of the storm screaming in my ears:

Monster,

Monster,

Monster.

I threw open the front door and hammered down the steps, racing out onto the sidewalk painted pale grayish-pink by the setting sun. My feet pounded the cement as I ran—as I sprinted, each of my violent footfalls seeming to echo those three words.

The storm had swallowed me—and there was nothing I could do to stop it.

I ran down the sidewalk and through the downtown, dodging reflections of my own silhouette in store windows until I finally reached that familiar place where the road curved away from the buildings and the noise. It was dark by the time I reached the trees. Their shadows stretched up to the gray sky, towering over me; their branches seemed to curve and clasp arms, blotting out everything else altogether until it felt like a dark tunnel that would never end.

But I kept running, every footfall rattling through my body like a tremor. Finally, I broke out onto the beach.

The sky was getting dark and I could already see the beginnings of starry pinpricks on the horizon stretched out over the lapping waves. I didn't stop; I didn't give myself time to second-guess. I pushed myself, running across the beach, heading straight for the water. My sneakers filled with the cold liquid, and it splashed up around my legs as I surged forward.

The freezing water knocked the air out of my lungs as soon as a wave slapped against my chest, followed by another and another until my clothes were like weights—drenched with the cold lake water that numbed my entire body until I couldn't feel a thing, not even the lapping of the water that was now up to my chest.

The dark line where the water met the sky blurred and ebbed far ahead of me, seeming to fade and reappear.

Come closer.

I pushed myself forward, wading in deeper until something stopped me. A sound above the lapping of the waves, a voice.

"Ion!"

I blinked, sucking in a trembling breath, wanting to look back but feeling too numb to move. My knees buckled beneath me, and the whooshing roar of water filled my ears as I slipped beneath the surface.

For a moment, everything was deafening, and then silent.

Then someone grabbed me by the hair. Sound came rushing back as I was yanked above the surface. I gasped for breath, kicking and writhing violently as two strong arms latched around my torso.

"Let me go!" My voice roared out of my throat, ragged and sounding like a stranger's. "Just let me die—just let me vanish!"

I felt the water parting around me as the powerful arms dragged me backward, through the waves and onto the beach again. I swung my arms, throwing blind punches, trying in vain to free myself.

"Ion, *stop!*" a voice finally shouted into my ear, slamming me down on the sand and pinning my arms to the ground. "Stop it!"

For a moment I just lay there gasping, staring up at the dark shape leaning over me. I had no idea who it was until my eyes began to slowly adjust to the low light. The glistening of his eyes was familiar.

The old man was soaked and panting for air. He looked down into my face, still holding me down.

"Do you give up that easily?" he shouted, breathless. "Do you quit before you've even begun?"

I stared up at him, still panting, still fighting against his grip. "You don't know anything about me—nothing!" I yelled up into his face. "You haven't been there; you don't know me! You have no idea what it's like to keep losing everything over and over again." My throat tightened and the air rushed out of my lungs in a sob. I squeezed my eyes shut. I didn't want to cry, but I couldn't seem to stop it. "To be something no one wants…"

"You are not *something*, Ion," the old man corrected me, his voice full of iron resolve. "You are *someone*."

"I'm a freak! I'm a monster—I can't—" I stammered and choked on the words that were burning in my throat. "I can't control it… I feel it growing stronger and stronger, and there's nothing I can do to stop it… No matter how hard I try, I can't stop it…"

The old man didn't say anything for a moment; then he released his grip on my hands. He helped me sit up and leaned in to look straight into my eyes.

"Ion, you are mistaken if you think I don't know," he said quietly. "That I haven't been there… that I haven't seen where you've come from or what you're going through…" He trailed off, almost as if he'd said too much.

I squinted at him through the darkness; my teeth began to chatter. "W-w-what do you mean?"

He didn't answer; he just studied my face for a moment before taking a steady breath. "You've never asked me how I know your name."

I stared at him, shivering. "I-I must h-have told you, didn't I?"

The old man shook his head. "You've never told me your name, Ion. And you've never asked me mine," he answered quietly. "You may not know who I am, Ion, but believe me… I know who you are and where you've come from." He paused. "And more importantly than that… I know where you're *going*."

A strange feeling filled me as I sat there, staring at him.

"Who are you?" I whispered.

The old man's expression didn't change; there was a glint in his eyes again.

"Someone you weren't supposed to meet yet," he answered quietly. "Someone who knows who you really are, and why you're afraid." He paused, still looking me in the eyes. "I know about everything that's been happening to you, Ion—*I know.*"

My heart was in my throat, beating hard and fast as I stared back at him. "But how? How can you know about any of it?"

The old man shook his head, his expression solemn. "It's not for you to know—not now, not yet."

In one violent motion I reached out and clasped his shoulder, my fingertips clutching on like he was the edge of a cliff and I was about to fall—again.

"Who are you?" I whispered, my voice cracking a little as I paused to rephrase, sucking in a sharp, shaking breath. "Who the hell am I?"

The old man's eyes stayed connected with mine for a long moment.

"One day I will answer both of these questions, Ion," he whispered, his tone serious. "But for now…"

He was the one to reach out a hand now. He pressed his first three fingers to the middle of my forehead in a triangle. My body instantly went numb; I felt paralyzed. The lapping of the waves and the brush of the wind faded away, leaving nothing but his voice— the last words he spoke. They echoed in the darkness as the world around me fell away.

"For now, you will forget you ever met me…"

SEVENTEEN

two months later

"ION? ION, ARE YOU LISTENING?"

The voice was distant, a muffled sound in the background of my thoughts. It drizzled in with the awareness of the sunlight drifting in through the window, leaving warm, golden patches across my face and staining my vision with afterimage silhouettes. Slowly, I began to refocus on the room around me: the tidy, corporate furniture scattered around the room, the nice social worker sitting in the chair across from me, holding a pen between her fingers. Her concerned brown eyes studied my face as she waited for an answer.

I squeezed my eyes shut and cleared my throat. "I, uh… Can you repeat the question, please?"

She seemed to contemplate my request for a moment, leaving the silence to take center stage again. Finally, she closed my composition notebook in her lap, smoothing her hands over the cover.

"Ion, I want you to know that I realize the past couple of months have been tough for you," she began, her voice raw and honest. "I know we've had to ask you a lot of questions. You've had to live in a few new homes, and you may not even really understand why all of this is happening to you."

"Because everyone thinks I'm dangerous," I retorted bluntly. "Because of what happened."

"It's not that we think you're dangerous, Ion," she assured me. "It's that we think you need help. There's a big difference."

"What are they going to do with me?"

"There's no need to worry about that right now."

I leaned forward a little, my heart beating a little faster now. "Please…"

Please.

"Just tell me," I pleaded, my voice raw. "Please."

She took a deep breath and let it out again. I could tell that whatever she was about to say would be real.

"Ion, the best option may be for you to live in a home that specializes in helping troubled youths."

The way she said it. The way she looked at me when she said it. I could tell it was already a sealed deal.

I didn't respond; I couldn't. I rubbed my hands over my face and swallowed back the lump that was beginning to form in my throat.

"Ion," she began again quietly, "I know it might feel like things have always been this way for you—or that it will always be this way…" She paused, looking at me. "But the truth is, everyone has a choice to either let go of their past or to allow it to define them. You don't have to let the things that have happened to you, or the things that you have done, become who you are."

My throat felt tight as I sat there looking at her.

"You still have your whole life ahead of you, Ion. You have a future—but you have to let go of the past so you can grab hold of it." Her fingers closed into a fist as if she had just snatched something valuable out of midair. "You don't have to be defined by what's happened."

I thought about what she was saying, pulling my gaze away from hers, my focus drifting to the window—to the light spilling in through the blinds. I could hear a bird singing outside, faintly, echoing in my head along with the earnest, hopeful words the woman sitting across from me had just spoken.

"It's not that I feel defined by what's happened." My answer came out quiet and cracked. "It's that I feel completely undefined… It's that I have no clue who the hell I am."

For a moment she said nothing. Her lips pressed into a sad smile; then she drew a fortifying breath and tapped the composition book still in her lap.

"That's what I'm here to help you with, Ion," she answered. "I want to help you. Let's go back to that question, alright?"

I swallowed, looking back down at my hands. My fingertips were trembling a little—not enough for her to notice, but I could feel it.

"The old man you wrote about," she began, looking back to my messy handwriting. "When did you first meet him?"

My gaze shifted back up to meet hers. I stared at her for a moment, repeating the question in my mind. There was something so strange and haunting and… familiar about the question. Yet, like a memory from a dream, I couldn't place it.

I stared at her for a long moment, confused. Finally I cleared my throat. "Old man?" I asked. "What old man?"

So the Journey Begins...

Continue Ion's story in the first book of *The Blood Race* series!

All Ion Jacobs ever wanted was to be normal. But when you're capable of killing with your very thoughts, it's hard to blend in with the crowd.

Running from his past and living in fear of being discovered, Ion knows he will never be an average college student. But when Hawk, the beautiful, mysterious girl next door unearths his darkest secret, Ion's life is flipped upside-down. He's shocked to discover a whole world of people just like him -- a world in another dimension, where things like levitation, shape-shifting, and immortality are not only possible... they're normal.

Forced to keep more secrets than ever before, Ion struggles to control his powers in the real world while commuting between realms -- until his arch enemy starts a fight he can't escape. Now he has sealed the fate of the Dimension, severing their connection to the real world, and locking himself inside forever. But a deadly threat hidden in plain sight may cost Ion more than just his freedom -- it may cost him his life.

WHAT READERS ARE SAYING:

"It made me think, left me gasping from truths, and nearly in tears over the raw, emotional power of the story. From the first word, I was swept away on a wild ride that I won't be forgetting anytime soon."

"I haven't read such an original story or one that completely captivated my attention in a long time. I'm intrigued, excited, scared, and more. And I have missed that feeling."

"*The Blood Race* doesn't shy away from controversial issues. I love the diversity of races, origins, and backgrounds in the characters, as well as the book's candor about struggles each of us face, such as temptation, deception, fear, and anger. The spiritual depth in this book is rare among young authors. I felt myself resonating with each word of wisdom spoken by Sensei, each truth that Hawk and Ion learn, each battle won. *The Blood Race* is a prime example of transformational fiction, entertaining but also expounding spiritual truth."

"This book is very fast paced and filled to the brim with beautifully written descriptions and great characters. Think X-Men meets Miss Peregrine, but in a fresh and exciting new twist. It reminded me of a modern, sci-fi, teenage Narnia."

"It is rare to find YA sci-fi with anything deeper than the surface as far as themes go (at least not good ones) and The Blood Race packed full of meaning and deeper layers while maintaining its integrity as a story."

ABOUT THE AUTHOR

When she's not hermiting away in her colorfully painted home office writing her next science fiction, passionate storyteller and adventurer Kate Emmons is probably on the road for a surf or hiking trip, listening to vinyls, or going for a power run. Emmons lives in the often-snowy hills of rugged Vermont with her husband and dog named Rocket.